All the Things We Leave Behind

Also by Riel Nason
The Town That Drowned

All the Things
We Leave
Behind

RIEL NASON

Edited by Bethany Gibson.
Cover and page design by Julie Scriver.
Cover image copyright © 2010 by Sarah Burnie.
Printed in Canada.
10 9 8 7 6 5 4 3 2 1

Library and Archives Canada Cataloguing in Publication

Nason, Riel, 1969-, author
All the things we leave behind / Riel Nason.

Issued in print and electronic formats.
ISBN 978-0-86492-041-6 (paperback).--ISBN 978-0-86492-731-6 (epub).--
ISBN 978-0-86492-927-3 (mobi)

I. Title.

PS8627.A7775A45 2016   C813'.6   C2016-902285-4
                                       C2016-902286-2

All the Things We Leave Behind is a work of fiction. Although many places mentioned
in the book do exist in New Brunswick, they appear here fictitiously with creative details
and descriptions. Other places, locations, names, characters, events, activities and
timelines are all a product of the author's imagination.

We acknowledge the generous support of the Government of Canada,
the Canada Council for the Arts, and the Government of New Brunswick.

Goose Lane Editions
500 Beaverbrook Court, Suite 330
Fredericton, New Brunswick
CANADA E3B 5X4
www.gooselane.com

For my Tess

Glory be to God for dappled things...
— Gerard Manley Hopkins, "Pied Beauty," 1877

Prologue

There is a boneyard deep in the woods. The deer and moose could show you where. They know the place that the trees stop and the carcasses begin. You could follow their cloven hoof prints. Walk past spruce and fir, tamarack, poplar and sugar maple. There is a dark path the does take to warn their fawns: this is what might come.

It is the Department of Transportation's boneyard. The many deer and few moose that are hit up or down the highway for almost two hundred miles are hauled in. The government men have a truck and trailer with hooks and chains and dark smears of blood. Over the years they have returned countless times to the pit, and the bodies have piled up.

The government men say they can sometimes feel the animals watching, hovering nearby in the forest, even if they can't see them. Or perhaps it is the presence of the ghost herd the men sense. People around here say it is hundreds strong, that there is a ghost for every deer or moose in the boneyard. There are bucks and does, bulls and cows, fawns, calves, glowing translucent white, sometimes suddenly charging, surging like a snow squall. The ghost herd has been blamed for countless close calls on our stretch of highway. Cars have swerved into the ditch or each other, the drivers later claiming to have seen an albino buck, or a group of deer going so fast they were only a pale blur in the headlights. The deer and moose spirits run back to the highway knowing they can't be killed again. People say it is the animals' revenge.

The boneyard's location is supposed to be secret, but hunters have stumbled on it over the years. The government men — the Undertakers — have talked too loud about it, when they're out drinking on Saturday nights. Or to find the boneyard yourself, you can listen for the circling crows and ravens.

I've always thought it's a place better left to the imagination. I'd never wanted to see the area's entire history of roadkill left to rot.

But I've been there.

By accident.

The first time was anyway.

I think I've finally learned to let it be.

SUMMER 1977

There's a little sign above the front door of our family business that says "Charles J. Davis and Son Antiques" in a fancy old-fashioned script, but no one seems to notice it and everybody calls the place The Purple Barn. It's just as well. The son, my brother Bliss, is missing, and Charlie J. and my mother are off searching, trying to find the path he took. I was left here alone and in charge. I'm not sure that promoting me to running the whole show was among Dad's best ideas ever, but my parents already have enough on their minds that they don't need anything except business-as-usual updates from me. I'll head inside soon and see how it goes. My parents left yesterday.

For now I'm sitting on a dark brown picnic table at the edge of the parking lot, watching the customers arrive. It can be pretty entertaining to see the tourists discover The Purple Barn for the first time. I know some of them are thinking, *What in the hell?* as they smile, shake their heads or roll their eyes. Almost everyone who pulls in off the highway has their car windows down. It's the first week of July, and it's already crazy skin-burning hot. Families dressed in shorts can't wait to escape from wood-panelled station wagons, to peel their legs from the vinyl seats. Kids lean ahead and perch their chins on their parents' shoulders.

"There it is!" a little boy might shout and point, his finger seeming to press the same imaginary button again and again.

Maybe his dad will glance to his mom and nod. "Well look what we've found here," he'll say. "Now isn't that the darndest thing?"

I get that The Purple Barn stands out from the rest. I know everything the tourists see en route to here, whether they entered New Brunswick from Quebec in the north, or further south at Houlton, Maine. That's the direction most people come from — starting up, travelling down. I've seen the Saint John River, its surface sparkling in the sun like a disco ball as it flows merrily alongside the highway, zigging and zagging. I've seen every view that makes travellers wonder which suitcase they packed their camera in and then second-guess if they brought enough film for the trip. I know the countryside — the forests, the fields. I've seen all the big white farmhouses and their newer neighbours, the few roadside motels, the Frosty Friend canteen in Meductic and the high Shogomoc bridge. I know the tourists passed by graffiti spray-painted on the shale left smooth when the rock was blasted out for the highway. They might have noticed that *Carl loves Lucy*, that the *RHS Class of '72 rules* and that *Bobby was here* (at least once).

Then, this:

An enormous rectangle, a hundred-foot-long barn, painted purple.

Really it's lilac or mauve, a rich purple softened a bit, like with a good dollop of white stirred in. It would be perfect for an Easter egg or eye shadow or an old lady's bathroom soap. The colour was mixed as a special order for a chain of ice cream stands in Maine. I don't know how the paint ended up at a flea market in Bangor any more than I understand why the border guard didn't wonder about my father and take him in for additional questioning when Dad admitted his true intention for bringing that sea of liquid lavender into the country. I mean, here is a building that looks like a giant version of a four-year-old girl's dream birthday cake.

My father used some of the leftover paint to make signs the tourists would have noticed on the way here too. The *signs* are purple arrows. The first one is upriver, almost to Florenceville. It's eight feet tall with "100 miles ahead" printed on it. There's another at 75 miles. Then 50, 25, 10, 5. People seeing them can't help but be curious. It's another reason I like to watch the tourists' reactions when they arrive. They know they're searching for something, they just don't know what.

Out in front of the barn are two tall telephone poles, spaced ten feet apart, with long pieces of plywood hammered across them, reading "Antiques," "Crafts," "Souvenirs," "Cold Pop" and — if anyone needs any further motivation — "Free Washrooms." There's a flower garden at the base of the giant sign. Pink rose bushes are surrounded by a wide ring of bright yellow marigolds and big rocks painted white. At the far side of the barn we have a little playground with a swing set, slide and teeter-totter. There are another eight picnic tables. Plus there's good old wide-open space — a huge lawn for people to stretch their legs, for kids to run around on. The Purple Barn is the Saint John River Valley's ultimate roadside attraction.

So I'm *officially* in charge of the store while my parents are gone, but my father's three employees are here to help me. There are two ladies: Mrs. Alvina Quinn (Quinny when she's out of hearing range), who is always — always — here, and Elizabeth, who works in the afternoons. I'm supposed to come in every day and make sure the place hasn't burned down or been robbed, a skunk or squirrel hasn't snuck in, or there's been no other bad-for-business emergencies. Other than that, I have the only key to The Room, where Dad keeps the inventory he's saved for his antique dealer friends. And I'm to talk to anyone who wants to sell us anything, whether it's someone clearing out their late aunt's attic, or one of Dad's two dump pickers, or Foster, the hermit who makes "folk art" furniture from bent twigs.

I know what I'm doing and I'm almost an expert on antiques from hanging around the store and listening to my father my whole life. I can rattle off statements like, "It's a late Victorian, Eastlake period piece, factory-made, ash, not oak, but excellent quality." I sometimes get raised eyebrows from customers when volunteering that type of information though, so I stick mainly to saying things about the weather. I'm seventeen — almost eighteen — and when it comes to antiques the shoppers would rather listen to what Quinny says, even if it's, "Goodness now, that is a lovely piece, isn't it? And it's got to be as old as the hills." Quinny has grey hair and wrinkles and considering she looks like she was alive when most of the stuff in the store was made, she's obviously well-informed.

Dean is the other employee. He's a year older than I am and is a friend of my brother's. He does all the things that would have been Bliss's job if he were here. Dean mows the grass, weeds the flower garden around the sign, picks up garbage, rakes the gravel in the parking lot and does all the heavy lifting. He helps tourists cram old dressers into the backs of their cars. He rearranges the furniture display to fill in the empty spot every time something sells. (Even if customers can't tell, it's always obvious to us when something is missing.) And Dean chats with me and tries to make me laugh — and sometimes kisses me.

Dean's my boyfriend.

I'm inside now, behind the counter with Quinny. We're positioned against the back wall so we have a decent view of the whole store. The inventory changes constantly but it's basically a mix of your grandparents' house and the entire contents of the Eaton's catalogue from seventy-five to a hundred years ago. Quinny's working the cash register and I'm putting the purchases in bags. She's already apologized to two customers for how slow I was wrapping newsprint around an amethyst vase and then this cookie jar shaped like a fat monk, which had "Thou Shall Not Steal – Cookies!" painted on his belly. Quinny's annoyed that I won't stand close enough to her that she can simply hand me an item without taking a step.

I'm not doing it to be a pain. I don't know how she's never figured it out, but no one can ever get too near her because of the force field that is her hair. She's Pentecostal, so every day she pins the half mile of silver tinsel that's never been cut into a flat bun on the top of her head. Except she teases it into a pouf first, so it sticks out as if she's hiding a tire under it. Her head is a mushroom in silhouette.

Quinny and I aren't exactly best buddies, but she has a good matronly hustle with the customers. She always wears skirts or dresses and is *pleasantly plump*, like she's obviously a good cook, who definitely bakes her own bread and probably even makes jams and jellies and at least three kinds of pickles. A real old-timey wholesome type whose opinion can be trusted. She makes quilts as well, which are for sale in the store, hanging down from the rafters. They're beautiful — huge patchwork spreads sewn with hundreds of tiny colourful pieces combined into all sizes of pinwheels and checkerboards and baskets of flowers. Quinny is a down-home superstar with the tourists. Mrs. New Brunswick. I think she's who people-from-away expect to meet when they get here.

A customer comes to the counter, a lady with a dark tan and bleached shoulder-length hair. She's carrying a pressed glass butter dish, carefully holding it in front of her with both hands. She smiles at me, then speaks to Quinny.

"I like this," she says. "A lot." The woman sets the dish down on the counter and traces a finger over one of the maple leaves in the pattern. "But I'm not sure I can convince my husband I need it." She glances back to the front door where a man with sunglasses and a shaggy grown-out perm stands smoking a cigarette, staring at the provincial road map we have posted on the wall.

"It's twenty-five, but I was wondering if you could do any better?" she asks.

"Well now," Quinny says. "The owner's not here and I'm afraid I really can't —"

"How about twenty?" I ask.

The woman looks at me, surprised, then double-checks with Quinny.

Once the purchase is made and the door is half-closed behind the woman, Mrs. Quinn adjusts her cat eye glasses, which everyone else stopped wearing when I was in elementary school, and looks at me with a slight yet intentional tilt of her head.

"You shouldn't be so careless with your father's money, Violet. If you'd been patient for just a moment she likely would have paid the twenty-five." Quinny smooths the front of her skirt, then neatly aligns the pen with the receipt book.

"Okay." I smile. It might look a little forced, but I'm aiming for natural. At least I know my new position as Quinny's superior hasn't affected our usual working relationship. Patience is definitely a virtue.

It's sunny when I go out the back door for a break, and as I squint the field becomes a blur of green — the daisies and brown-eyed Susans blending into the tall grass. There's a path I take, that Bliss and I have taken for years, to the forest. There are about four acres of meadow, a sprawling square before the treeline starts. I slip my sandals off and leave them halfway down the path. The dirt is hard-packed and warm beneath my feet. The sun is shining almost directly overhead and I can feel it on the part in my hair, my nose, my shoulders. On the surface of my arms freckles are germinating like seeds.

I'm almost to the edge of the woods when I hear, "Miss Davis! Miss Davis!"

As I turn around, Dean rushes up to me. He takes off his ball cap and wipes his forehead with his sleeve. He has dark blond hair and grey eyes. He's pretty cute, even with his new addition of a moustache that, for now, looks like little more than a baby's eyebrow.

"As your humble employee," he takes my hand and kisses it, "I wanted to see if there was any way I could help make your debut as big boss lady go more smoothly. May I assist you with your break?"

The nut. He's grinning.

"Good one. But you know what?" I say. "I think I'm going to take this one solo." I hope he's not disappointed since we usually sit back here together.

He doesn't miss a beat. "Figures," he says. "I knew the power would go straight to your head."

I shrug.

He studies my face. He looks like he's about to turn serious and ask me if I'm really doing okay.

"Back to work then!" I command and point at the barn. "On the double!"

He gives me a quick kiss on my lips, then runs.

It's cooler in the woods. The old trees are well-spaced, but they are tall, looming, with wide-spread branches. The stands of poplar and birch are mixed in with the evergreens. Alder bushes grow here and there along with bunches of ferns grouped like bouquets. I once saw a red trillium on the forest floor.

I walk about twenty more feet to a stream and step knee-deep into it. There's green moss on the rocks on the bottom. I reach into the water and lift an old brick off an upside-down antique wire egg basket that I use to keep my pop bottles well submerged, icy-cold and safely anchored in place. I grab an Orange Crush and use the opener I leave tucked in the hole of a fallen log. I brush a few pieces of old man's beard moss and a light dusting of fresh pine needles off my canvas lawn chair before I sit down to drink my pop. A crow flies over and caws out a warning that I'm here. The longer I sit, the quieter it seems to get around me. The sounds of the traffic on the highway — the transport trucks and cars and campers — the voices of customers in the parking lot and kids in our little playground all fade to a distant hum. My body temperature lowers.

I close my eyes. I slept horribly last night. I don't remember dreaming, and I'm sure I wasn't asleep for more than twenty minutes at a time. I'd love to be able to drift off, even for a little bit. I tuck both hands under my thighs to help keep myself still. I tilt my head back against the top of the chair and try my best to think of nothing except being here, now. And it almost works.

As I walk back across the field, I see the woman who bought the butter dish and her husband sitting at one of the picnic tables with a cooler, finishing a late lunch. Quinny was right, the woman definitely would have paid the full twenty-five dollars. It's pretty easy to tell when someone really wants something. Dad says that if you look carefully, desire is a hard thing for people to hide and you can see it in their eyes. I saw the lady imagining the butter dish in use this Thanksgiving, right there on her dining-room table beside the baked squash, impressing her mother-in-law. I knew she wasn't going to walk away without her treasure for the sake of five dollars. (If only all mind-reading were that easy.) But there's nothing wrong with giving deals — especially to the tourists. My father says that if you give them a good deal on the trip down, chances are they'll stop in and spend the rest of their money on the trip back. Besides, I know Dad paid a grand total of a dime for that butter dish at a yard sale up in Woodstock.

By the end of my first day in charge of the store, both the building and Quinny are still standing. I hop in the store's Ford half-ton — it's blue, not purple — roll both windows down, and after waiting a good while for a break in the traffic, turn out of the barn parking lot. I drive to Seven Birches Campground and Cabins. It's where I'm staying for the summer.

It's barely a half mile down the highway from The Purple Barn, on the opposite side, near the river. Seven Birches, The Purple Barn, and about fifteen houses make up the rural community of Hawkshaw. The campground has a hundred sites, along a dozen or so winding gravel drives, all with water hookups and electricity. There are a lot of trees, the birches you'd expect —but way more than seven, probably about seventy now — as well as some evergreens, so there's shade and protection from rain for the campers, but not so many you'd feel you were sleeping in the forest. There's a store/canteen called The Snack Shack, a playground with horseshoe pits, a pool, a building with washrooms and showers, and a big campfire circle with log benches.

Twelve cabins sit in a row. My parents rented one for me for the summer. It looks the same as the other eleven. It's stained the colour of burnt gingerbread and has a little porch with a white spindle railing and fancy white icing trim above the large front window. There are two high back yellow rockers (each cabin has a different colour) on the porch, with enough clearance to rock as long as they are at an angle.

The river is just beyond the Hawkshaw Road, which is the loop you drive down from the highway, really only about forty feet away. The highway is behind the campground, up a slight hill.

The cabin has two bedrooms, and my friend Jill is staying with me. Both our families live in Riverbend, on the other side of the river. It's a small town, 1,027 people. The exact number is posted on the "Welcome" sign because it's not hard to keep count. It only takes five minutes to drive from Riverbend over to The Purple Barn. I could be staying at our house, but Mom and Dad didn't want me in the big empty place all by myself.

For supper I get an order of fries from The Snack Shack, and then I take a walk around to see who showed up for the night. I read the licence plates of cars and campers as I go. It's an old habit. Bliss got me started after Mom started him. When The Purple Barn first opened, Mom worked with Dad. That meant Bliss and I went to the store too and that we had to entertain ourselves for the day. We could hang out in the storage room and colour or read, or go to the playground, or run around in the meadow and along the forest's edge. We only had each other as playmates. The Purple Barn was the place we spent the most time together. And there was plenty to keep us busy — still, sometimes Mom came up with special projects for us.

One morning the summer that I was eight and Bliss was nine, Mom took our crayons and drawing book from the storage room and led us to the parking lot. Among the New Brunswick cars, there was one from Pennsylvania. Its licence plate said "Keystone State." After my mother made a big production of checking that there was no one in the car and we wouldn't be backed over, she knelt down near the rear bumper. She took a dark blue crayon from the box and peeled all the paper off the outside. Then she ripped a sheet from the drawing book and smoothed it over the licence plate. She rubbed the crayon back and forth as we watched the numbers appear. She worked carefully until the whole outline of the plate and the numbers and words were transferred onto the paper. I thought it was pretty cool, but Bliss stared like Mom had created a masterpiece. .

We went inside and Bliss coloured the background of the paper licence plate orange, exactly the same as the one on the car, then cut it out. He wanted to go right back to the parking lot and do another. Someone from North Carolina had pulled in. Their licence plate was white and red and said "First in Freedom." Bliss got his third one right before we went home for the day. A camper from New Hampshire arrived. Its green-and-white plate said "Live Free or Die."

By the next Saturday, Bliss had a scrapbook to glue his paper licence plates in. I became his lookout, standing by the driver's side door. I promised I'd always be sure he was safe as he did the rubbing.

We pretended we had walkie-talkies. "All clear? Safe to go, Vi?" Bliss would say without looking up at me. "Over." I'd reply, "Roger," and he'd say, "Roger, Roy Rogers," because he thought it was funny. (He knew the name because Dad's childhood Roy Rogers's lunchbox was in our garage, filled with spare nails now.)

Bliss was always excited to see a car from a faraway province or state. There were probably thirty cars from New Brunswick, Quebec, Ontario or Maine for every one from anywhere else. Near the end of the summer when he got a rubbing of a Northwest Territories licence plate, which was shaped like a polar bear, he glued it on the cover of his scrapbook. He went through crayons so fast you'd have thought he was snacking on them. Sometimes travelling in our own car we'd quiz each other about what licence plate slogans matched up with what places: where is the "Land of 10,000 Lakes?" (Minnesota); what is the "Sunshine State?" (Florida).

He added to his licence plate collection the next two summers. Even when Mom didn't have to work with Dad very often and we only went to the store now and then, Bliss and I would scan the parking lot. But by the time he was twelve, he didn't look at, or add to, the five scrapbooks anymore. They stayed on a shelf in his room.

He might have simply grown bored with the whole thing, but when I look back now, I also think that all those licence plates from other places reminded him that everyone else was moving, travelling, having summer adventures, while we stayed put. We stopped talking about using the scrapbooks as a checklist for all the provinces and states we'd visit one day. We stopped scheming about the big road trip we'd go on when we got older — just Bliss and me, taking turns driving. We used to talk about it for hours, planning every little detail: where we'd stop to eat, how much money we'd need for everything, who we'd send postcards to. I always figured we'd go though — eventually. Never once did he say he'd changed his mind about us exploring together. Never once did I imagine that he'd go off without a word, without me.

Jill is getting out of her boyfriend's truck when I get back to the cottage. Johnny's window is down and his eight-track is blaring. I don't recognize the song, but he's singing along and playing the steering wheel, using his fingers as drumsticks.

Johnny beeps and waves and Jill turns in my direction. She's in full Victorian dress, wearing a long-sleeved rust-coloured floral blouse with puffs at the shoulders and a full-length brown skirt shaped by a significant bustle. We laugh a lot about her bustle, which is a required part of her costume as a tour guide at Kings Landing Historical Settlement. It's basically a pillow she ties around her waist to make her rear end look bigger.

"Hey, foxy lady," I say.

"Oh, you know it." She does a quick twirl and her skirt lifts enough to reveal her black lace-up shoes bought from the army surplus in Fredericton. "Listen, I'm just grabbing my clothes from inside. Go hop in the truck. Johnny's parents are having a barbecue."

"I already ate."

"Doesn't matter. Come anyway. What else are you doing?"

I should probably go. I look at Johnny in the truck, then past him to the river.

"No," I say. "I'm cool. It was really busy at the store today and I'm pretty beat."

Jill stares at me for a few seconds. "Vi," she says.

"Jill."

"Viiii," she raises her eyebrows slightly as she speaks. "We're going to have a fun summer. Good times, right? I promised you that. And you promised me you'd try."

"I know. And we will. Really."

Johnny beeps the horn again. Jill swats the air in his direction.

"Okay, one night's grace," she says. "One — that's it. Stay here if you want for now, but after this I'm going to insist. Okay?" Jill looks right at me, waits for me to nod. Then she dashes inside, changes, comes out in a red tube top and shorts and leaves with Johnny.

I sit on the yellow porch rocker and look out at what the Seven Birches brochure calls a "scenic river view." Right in front of me is a wide stroke of blue. It is beautiful here. It's easy to understand why the old New Brunswick licence plates said "Picture Province."

I stay outside for a long time, until the sun finally starts to set. I think about my day. I let my mind wander back to me sitting on the picnic table in the parking lot, alone at the forefront of our family's business.

I was seven when I first saw The Purple Barn. One Sunday afternoon, my father said we were going on a family drive that would end with a special surprise. I knew it was a big deal when Mom brought her camera and Dad told Bliss to make sure I didn't peek out from under the scarf that was tied over my eyes. We seemed to drive for a long time, and I had no idea where we might be going or why. When we arrived, Bliss helped me out of the back seat and led me to the middle of the parking lot.

"You're going to love it, Vi," he whispered and squeezed my hand. "This is what Dad and I have been working on."

"All righty then," my father said. "Go ahead."

I took off the scarf.

"We painted it violet for you, Violet," Bliss said.

I stared.

Then I looked to Mom, Dad, Bliss. They were grinning as if they'd performed a magic trick. And in my seven-year-old mind they had. Dad winked at Mom. I grabbed Bliss and hugged him tight. I felt like everything inside me was jumping for joy and that pushed a burst of laughter from my chest. Soon I was giggling and couldn't stop. Dad said I wasn't just tickled pink about the barn, but tickled purple. It was the most clever thing I'd ever heard.

So that's another reason — my memory of that glorious little-kid glee — why I like to see other people discover The Purple Barn. Maybe something will click in my brain and it will seem as if I'm back there again, living that moment, making that perfect connection. I'd love to be able to summon the fullness of that wonderful feeling at will, distill it and keep it in an elegant old perfume bottle, an atomizer. I might spritz a little, or else spray and spray it as thick as fog and breathe it all in.

I wonder where my parents are now.

And Bliss, where are you now?

2

As beautiful as the river is, it's hiding something. The Saint John River is a lot bigger than it used to be. It was once a skinnier, twisted strip, really just a stream in some places. Then the government built a dam at Mactaquac, about fifteen miles downriver from here, and the entire landscape changed. There was a giant permanent flood. The water swallowed a whole town called Haventon. It happened ten years ago when I was still a kid. We lived in Fredericton then.

The river more than doubled in width, and everything — houses, farms, schools, churches — sitting along the water's edge had to be moved out of the way or torn down. Jill's grandmother's house had to be moved. The old school was demolished. Some people burned their homes. It's a strange thing to think about, hard to imagine how it used to be.

It's also how my father came into what he calls the best opportunity of his life.

Dad's always been an antique dealer, but his store in Fredericton was never as big as he wanted. He also made about ninety per cent of his money between April and October but couldn't board up the place for the five slow months, since it was right downtown. He used to complain to my mother about having to sit around half the year with his thumb up his ass.

At first he tried to buy an old church out here. Plans for the new highway to be built less than twenty-five feet in front of it had the congregation concerned that the sound of transport trucks rumbling by might drown out their hymns and prayers. They were going to sell and build new. Until it was decided — according to Dad — that it was somehow unholy for antiques to be sold in a former place of worship, and they tore the church down instead. (Although they didn't mind that he bought all the pews to sell to people to use in their houses as benches. Plus the fancy chair that was at the front for the minister is now in my parents' bedroom, and I know — due to poor timing once on my part — that my father sits on it every morning in his underwear to pull on his socks.)

The barn was once part of a big farm. The house that went with it was in the flood plain and couldn't be moved so it was burned. But the barn was nearer the back of the property, conveniently aligned along the new highway route. It's way bigger than the church and Dad bought it for next to nothing. Sure he spent money cleaning and renovating it, getting gravel for the parking lot and buying the picnic tables and swing set and sign outside, but he says that, all in all, it couldn't have turned out any better.

I'm the first one to arrive at The Purple Barn. I woke at four-thirty, and since lying in bed fantasizing about Mom and Dad miraculously finding Bliss at the first place they stop didn't help me go back to sleep, I got up. It's a little after eight now and the store doesn't open until nine.

The sun is strong and it's warm already. Lots of travellers are on the road, off to an early start. The highway gets busier as July progresses, filling with big campers that drive slowly and accumulate long lines of cars behind them. There are very few passing lanes along the whole stretch of the river valley, and with this much traffic it is nearly impossible to squeeze by anyone. I bet a lot of drivers get in a bad mood — hot, bothered, swearing, all the while just wanting to speed along to make the next PEI ferry. I think sometimes people pull in to the store simply for a break from the highway frustration.

I park the truck at the back of the barn and head to the meadow. I pick a big bunch of daisies, red devil's paintbrushes, goldenrod and bits of timothy. Inside I change the flowers in the six vases we currently have arrangements in and add three more — one in a carnival glass vase and two in stoneware ginger beer bottles. Then I start moving around some of the small things in the store. I don't move furniture, but I take glass, china, kitchenware, toys and books and shuffle them from one shelf to another. I set a few things on the tops of tables and dressers. It doesn't matter what goes where, only that I specifically choose a few special objects to put somewhere new. Dad does it all the time and says it's a secret sales strategy.

Once an item has been touched, admired, selected, desired by one person, then other people are drawn to it too. It's as if it has an invisible seal of approval, a little bit of endorsement that can somehow be sensed. Often when one customer almost buys something, can't decide — yes, no, yes — then ultimately puts it back and leaves, the next person through the door will pick it up and buy it. My father says there's an innate human desire to want something other people want. To covet. It doesn't have to be thy neighbour's wife. It can be thy dead grandmother's candy dish.

Mrs. Quinn is the only person I know who drives with her headlights on during the day (she thinks it's safer), so it's easy to spot her when she pulls in off the highway. She parks her old robin's-egg-blue Ford LTD out front like Dad asks her to, because it makes it look like we're open and already have a customer.

When she comes inside, she brings a new quilt, which she unfolds on the counter. It's red and white with an enormous star made of diamonds. I don't know how she makes her quilts so fast. I'm sure she's the type who believes that the devil finds work for idle hands, but really, she must sit at her sewing machine every second she's not at the store. I get the ladder to hang the quilt from the rafters. I fold it carefully so it's draped above the cash register like a guiding star. It sells at ten thirty.

A couple from New York take all of two seconds to decide. The woman looks up and says, "You know, that blanket's quite lovely." The man says, "Would you like it?" The woman says, "Yes, I think I would." They pay cash.

I can tell Quinny's thrilled; it's a new record. She phones her husband to tell him about it the second the couple are out the door.

Elizabeth arrives at noon and brings my lunch. She's less than half Quinny's age and she's married and has a little girl named Michelle. When Elizabeth works at the store in the afternoons, Michelle stays with her grandmother. Elizabeth brings me a warm meal on a real plate — an extra serving of whatever she makes at home. She volunteered to do it when my father told her that he and Mom would be away. She said it was her way to help out. I could certainly make my own sandwich, but she was insistent. And really, peanut butter on bread is no match for a square of baked macaroni and cheese with a nice crunchy crust and a homemade biscuit.

The store has a steady stream of customers until around three o'clock. We sell several old dishes and framed prints, some silverware, two child's chairs and a baby-blue crocheted toilet paper holder shaped like a poodle from our craft section. When there's finally a lull, Dean comes and grabs me for a break so today I won't slip away without him. He helps a customer in the parking lot load a wicker plant stand into her car, and then we head to the forest's edge.

I think it's the hottest day of the year so far. There's no breeze. There isn't the slightest ripple in the timothy in the field as we walk along the path. A crow is perched on a tree in the distance. It has its beak open, trying to stay cool. As we reach the forest's edge, another crow flies to the same tree as the first and opens its beak too. It looks as if the birds are silently screaming. You'd think there was something wrong with them if you didn't know what they were doing.

I get a pop for each of us from my stash, and we sit side by side at the stream's edge. I pick up a twig and swish it around in the water.

Dean tells me about a customer that he overheard talking to her friend. She pointed at a large white ironstone chamber pot and said she had one exactly like it at home.

"Claims it's just perfect to serve her potato salad in," Dean says and grins.

"Yuck," I say.

But I think Dean was hoping I'd laugh. He takes a long drink of his Sprite and finishes the bottle.

"You haven't heard from your parents yet, have you Vi?"

I shake my head and watch the bubbles that form in the water underneath the twig as I move it.

"Did they say which way they were going? Did they start through the States or up through Quebec? I suppose Bliss could've started out either way. Right? You know —" He looks at me and stops himself. He puts his arm around my shoulders.

"They'll figure it out. Give it a bit and I'm sure your dad will call soon." He kisses my forehead. "At the very least he'll want to make sure Quinny hasn't tried to overthrow you."

"Yeah, ha, ha," I say.

I go in to tell Quinny I'm leaving for the day. (As long as three bus tours don't all show up at once and the line to buy things is out the door, my hours are up to me.) The phone is ringing. I can see her already hurrying towards the counter to get it, her skirt flapping. I try not to hope that it's my father. Most of the time when anyone calls here it's to sell us something. Like someone found some ancient clunky typewriter in the back corner of their shed and then you have to ruin their fantasies of fortune by saying they may as well use it as an anchor for their boat as drag it over here. A good call is when someone has inherited a family home and they want my father to buy out the whole place. But as determined as I am to do the best job I can while my parents are gone, the last thing I want to be involved in on a scorching-hot summer day is scrounging through someone's muggy, stale attic, all the while waiting to be attacked by resident mice, bats or overheated raccoons.

I stop by the brochure rack to listen as Quinny picks up the phone.

I can tell right away by the tone of her voice that it's not Dad. After a bit she says, "Oh, yes. Yes, that's what we do here. Certainly. I'll have to let you talk to our shop expert, Miss Davis. She'll be able to give you more information." Quinny is smiling as she talks.

Since it's obvious from what I've heard of the conversation that the call must be something along the lines of Operation Attic, this is my cue to leave. I slip out the front door before Quinny looks up. If she is going so far as to generously claim me as "our shop expert" it definitely sounds like something that can wait until tomorrow.

I see Jill at a distance lying on the tiny riverfront beach made of trucked-in sand as I open the front window of the cottage. She's trying to get a tan. She's outside all day at Kings Landing, but she's always covered. She even has a straw hat that she keeps in place with a lethal-looking hat pin. People say to her about every fifteen minutes, "You must be hot," but she tells them you get used to it. Then she smiles and poses with them for pictures, which also happens about every fifteen minutes.

Jill sometimes says that the KLHS of Kings Landing Historical Settlement actually stands for Kinda Like High School. It's pretty fun, but there's also a lot to learn. The staff have a thick training manual full of historical facts and dates to memorize. Jill gives tours so she really has to know the material backwards and forwards and be prepared for questions. It's like a history test she takes every day and needs to make a hundred per cent on. She's officially called an *interpreter* because she presents information about the lives of people from a century ago in a way that's easy to understand. We sometimes joke about it. I think a lot of people could use an *interpreter* to make their own life easier to understand.

My father thinks Kings Landing is Disney World — New Brunswick style anyway. He always bought a family season's pass when we were younger. We'd sometimes go on Sundays, the one day the store was closed, and look together through the houses, barns, blacksmith shop, church, sawmill, school and store. But after a while, Mom and Dad would stop for an apple cider at the King's Head Inn and just Bliss and I would explore. There are animals in the barns: horses and cows, pigs and sheep, chickens and cats. You can watch the sawmill's massive working water wheel from a long bridge platform, so you're virtually over top of it. There are paths to run on through fields and little bits of forest.

I can understand why Jill doesn't mind working there. If we didn't have the antique store, I'd probably work there too. Jill's been my friend since I was little, since we first came here, and it's funny how we both ended up with jobs centred around life in the past. Sometimes it's not so bad living in the past.

. . .

I stop by The Snack Shack. Dwayne, the owner of Seven Birches, is behind the counter. He's a big man with dark hair and an auburn and grey moustache. He's doing a crossword puzzle but sets down his pen when he sees me.

"How's the antiques biz?" Dwayne asks.

"Oh, you know, same old, same old," I repeat Dad's standard pun. "How about you? You booked full every night now?"

"Pretty much. And I just rented another cabin for the summer. Right next to yours actually. Some young guy by himself. Paid cash for the first two weeks right up front. You might —"

The screen door swings open.

Dwayne half nods and glances sideways. The guy who comes in looks like he's in his early twenties. He's got shoulder-length brown hair. He's wearing sunglasses, which he leaves on. In my peripheral vision I see him go to the white kitchen fridge that says "Pop and Milk Inside."

"So you're doing all right," Dwayne asks, picking up our conversation again. "And your mom and dad got off on their vacation okay?"

"All good," I say.

The guy comes up to the counter with a can of Coke. He pays Dwayne then pulls off the tab to open it. He's about to toss the tab in the garbage can.

"You know you have to join that on the chain," I say. I point up.

Dwayne has long chains of hooked-together pop tabs criss-crossing the ceiling. He's added to them for years. Kids love to hook and fold their tabs on the loose end that Dwayne keeps dangling near the cash. There could be a mile of linked tabs up there winding back and forth like a shiny silver spider web above us. It's really something to see it twinkle when the sun shining through the front window hits it just right.

"It's an unofficial rule around here," I smile. "I think you even get to make a wish or something, right?" I look at Dwayne.

Dwayne laughs.

"Oh, okay, here." The guy flicks me the tab before he goes back out the door. I don't catch it and it makes a little tinkling sound as it hits the floor. The screen door slams.

"Don't worry about him," Dwayne says. "He wasn't exactly Dale Carnegie when he checked in either. He's probably just from Toronto."

"That's my neighbour?"

"Well, for a while anyway. Doesn't seem the tourist type but who knows."

"Yeah." I pick up the pop tab and hook it on the end of the chain. I ping it with my finger and watch it swing.

3

Bliss and I sometimes sat on the picnic table out front and watched for cars with lobster traps on their roof racks. Mom suggested it the first time and we thought it was a joke, but sure enough, within ten minutes, we saw a trap secured on top of a big sedan, ready to catch any flying lobsters that were swooping down too close to the highway. One day we counted twenty-three traps in less than an hour. Another time we saw a station wagon with a stack of five; Bliss guessed there must be one for each family member. They seemed to be the ultimate New Brunswick souvenir that tourists simply could not return home without.

Quinny said once, in a tone that implied she knew of such things, that nautically themed decorating was increasingly popular with the well-to-do. That many "dens" and young boys' rooms were done up that way. (I think she read about it in one of her *Family Circle* magazines that she buys from the rack near the cash at the Riverbend Save-Easy.) I bet a lot of lobster traps end up in basements and garages. But once I did overhear a tourist tell my mother that the three traps he'd picked up in Shediac were for his wife to make some sort of display in her flower garden. In Saskatchewan.

. . .

"You're late, Violet," Quinny says from behind the counter as soon as I swing open the store's front door. You missed two important calls."

I look up at the clock. It's ten fifteen. Really? That seems impossible. I left the campsite just before nine. I guess I let my mind wander a little too far for too long while I was sitting out front, watching the cars pull in.

"Sorry," I manage. "Was it Dad?"

"Well," Quinny says, "first it was the same woman as yesterday. The one I was talking to as you darted away." Quinny pushes her glasses up from where they've slid down her nose. The gesture is so purposeful and performed with such a direct glare at me, that I realize if I'd been her child I would have had a lot of spankings. "She has an entire estate to sell. She's from away, but it's an old family place, in the area somewhere. And on your father's behalf, I most certainly said we were interested. She'll be phoning again soon with the details and to set up a time."

"And the other call?"

"Yes, your father, Violet. He was extremely disappointed to have missed you. I mentioned the estate, and he said you're to immediately ask Mr. Kensey if he'll go with you to see it. You're to ask him today. No excuses. Also, your father wants you to do a quick check on the house. He'll be phoning again tomorrow."

Mr. Kensey is Foster Kensey the woods-dwelling hermit — the folk artist. His three-legged twig tables with hearts on the front are among the store's best-selling items.

I scan the store. There are about ten customers.

"Should I go now?" I ask.

"Yes, Violet. I've certainly been fine so far this morning without you," Quinny replies.

A peaceful walk in the woods will be nice.

. . .

It's cool in the forest. I'm following the stream to find my way to Foster's. It will take a full half-hour to walk to his place. I don't wander — not because I'm scared of getting lost, but because Foster sets traps for fox and who knows what else. They are leg traps with a toothy jaw ready to spring and bite. A guy from school got caught in a trap when he was a child and we heard he had to get his whole foot sewn back on. (I obviously know it wasn't that extreme, but it must have been bad.) Even at seventeen he has a dark red scar around his ankle, like when your socks are too tight and the top leaves an imprint even after you take them off.

Foster has lived in the woods behind The Purple Barn since the store first opened. He and my father have some sort of agreement. The Purple Barn used to be the Kensey family's barn. Foster is the one Dad bought it from back when the dam was built and the area was flooded. Foster kind of came with the property. Dad's big joke to Mom was, "You know, free hermit with purchase." The government expropriated the house Foster had grown up in. His parents were dead and he was living there alone. The word around here was that Foster was already a loner and not a big fan of the government to begin with. Losing the house was the final straw for him; Foster saw it as the ultimate verification of the government's uselessness and his justification to go off the grid.

He built a cabin in the woods. And he's way back there, probably well beyond what was once his land, probably squatting on Crown land. *So there.* Not just woods, but backwoods. Living the wild life. Or living with the wildlife. I've wondered if he finds it strange to see the barn painted purple, all done up with fancy furniture and shelves of pretty glass where piles of hay and mounds of manure once were, but I've never asked him.

Bliss was always sent to deliver messages to Foster or to help haul in his latest creations. Every couple of weeks, Foster would bring a bunch of twig furniture loaded on a homemade skid he dragged behind him. Bliss would follow along, making sure nothing fell off or got snagged on a tree branch. Dad only takes twenty per cent of what Foster's twiggy artworks sell for, so for a hermit he has pretty good cash flow. I don't know that he spends much of it though, except for the most basic groceries every few months.

It might seem fair to ask how Dad came to choose Foster as my chaperone. I mean, here I am traipsing through the forest to go ask a hermit who lives without running water or electricity to help represent Charles J. Davis and Son Antiques to some lady we've never met.

But it's exactly due to the fact that Foster's a recluse that my father wants him to go. As Dad says, Foster doesn't give a sweet shit about what my father buys, who he buys it from and, most importantly of all, what he pays for it. Foster doesn't gossip — and he has no one to gossip to even if the urge struck. Dad makes a lot of money, sometimes with a profit margin that would make people around here faint. When dealers who sell antiques in Toronto or New York buy things from The Room, they recognize the freshly picked treasures (locally known as junk) and are willing to pay the price. My father's worked years to build up his expertise and learned to distinguish the best from the rest. He has earned other dealers' respect. But dealing in antiques locally is a dangerous public relations game, since your neighbours are both your suppliers and your customers.

I can see Foster sitting in front of his cabin in a huge twig-art throne. The back of it is probably eight feet high. He's twisted twigs to make several hearts framed by fancy loops and braids, then at the top there's a buck in profile with two big antlers. I'm sure the chair would get snapped up immediately if we ever had it for sale in the store. Foster looks like the King of the Forest, dressed in a green-and-black checkered coat. He's reading a book.

In the rest of the cleared area, which is about forty feet square, is a cut-down metal barrel that Foster has been using as a fireplace and a wide lean-to frame with dangling furs and skins. A little garden is in the middle of the clearing where the most sunlight comes through. There's a galvanized tub, a large double-handled copper boiler, two more barrels which are likely to collect rain, and three other, plainer twig chairs. The cabin itself is small, not much bigger than our living room, but it also has a covered porch extending out front. It's solid looking, made with thick logs and real shingles on the roof. There are two smaller buildings behind it — probably an outhouse and some sort of shed.

Foster doesn't look up until I'm within three feet of him. But I'm sure he sensed me in the breeze long ago and probably heard me coming for the past ten minutes, crunching dead leaves under my feet. He puts his finger on his place on the page.

"Violet, what brings you to this neck of the woods?" I think he's smiling slightly, but he has such a big moustache and beard it's hard to tell. "Let me get you a beer," Foster says before I respond. I can't say I was expecting that. But Foster's the last person to care about any government regulations, so I'm sure it makes no difference to him that I'm a year and a smidge short of legal.

He gets up and sets his book on the chair. It's *The Blue Castle* by Lucy Maud Montgomery. Foster's very well read. Dad lets him use the store as his personal library and take whatever he wants — as long as he brings it back. Foster walks to the side of his cabin, moves three large rocks, lifts first a big old tin Sussex Ginger Ale sign and then an antique six-panel door off the ground. They are the lids on his makeshift refrigerator. He jumps down into the hole he's just uncovered, which is so deep only his head and shoulders show above it. In a few minutes he comes back with a Schooner for me. There's still a little snow stuck to the bottom of his boot, snow that's probably been packed down in his fridge since April. The beer is even colder than the pop I keep in the stream. Foster drags another twig chair over. It's surprisingly comfortable, nothing poking where it shouldn't.

I drink slowly. It's good. Not only the taste but the feeling. A wonderful calm washes over me. The forest is quiet all around us. The sun is bright and high in the sky, filtering down through the branches of the poplars and evergreens.

"Anything exciting happen out here lately?" I finally ask.

"I saw your brother's deer the other day," Foster says.

"Speckles? Are you sure?"

"Pretty hard to mistake the old fella. Walked right through my yard here."

"Yeah," I say. "Yeah, of course. I just hadn't seen him in so long. I thought maybe he — I thought maybe he wasn't still around."

I take another sip of beer. I look across Foster's clearing to the forest beyond.

"So you come out here to ask me for a date or what?" Foster smooths his hair at the part. "Where we off to?" Dad had told Foster that if a buying trip came up, I'd be out to ask for his help.

"Next week probably. I don't know where the place is yet. I'm just checking that you're not going on vacation or anything."

"I'll be here."

He picks up his book and starts reading.

I wait. I finish my beer and put the empty bottle on the chair. Foster doesn't look up again.

"Okay, well, see you then," I say. "Foster."

He nods ever so slightly. I turn to go.

He laughs. I look back and realize it's because of whatever he's reading. He's already back in the story, oblivious to every other thought or thing around him. Must be nice.

. . .

I'm in no hurry to get back since Quinny made it obvious she had everything under control at the barn. I walk to the edge of the stream and sit on the ground. I lean against a fallen log; I can feel the rough bark strong and solid against my back. I stretch my legs long in front of me and close my eyes. I can smell mud and damp leaves. The faint squeak of tree branches shifting against each other high above me and the water slipping over rocks are all I hear. I'm not sure how long I sit before I sense I'm being watched. I sit up and look around, but no one's there. A slight breeze blows and lifts the ends of my hair.

I close my eyes again and take a deep, even breath. But the feeling comes back. This time when I look there's a doe. A brown white-tailed deer is upstream at the water's edge. She's perfectly still and she's looking at me. Even from this distance her eyes are so soft and dark and full, trimmed with thick black lashes. Her fur is the colour of butterscotch. Her legs are thin and sleek, and strong. But then, with the slightest shift of my body, as I straighten myself to see her better, the doe is startled and gone.

Which is exactly the instinct a deer should have. Running back to its own kind with leaps and bounds, snapping fallen branches as it goes. Away from me.

It's how Speckles should have acted the first time Bliss and I saw him, seven or eight years ago, along this same stream. It was late spring, and Bliss and I were picking the few fiddleheads we could find. Bliss looked up and saw Speckles about twenty feet away.

"Violet. Vi, look," Bliss whispered. "Down there." He raised his chin in the direction of the buck.

The deer's face, neck, front legs and about two-thirds of its belly were solid white, but the rest of it was splattered with brown dots and splotches as if it had splashed through a mud puddle. At first, I thought it was some sort of strange deer that had changed white for the winter, like a rabbit or ermine, and was still in the process of changing back to brown.

"Can you believe it?" Bliss said. "What are the chances?"

"Is it an albino?" I asked.

"I don't know. I don't think he can be an albino with those brown speckles. But look at him. He's amazing."

The buck stared at us as we considered him. He didn't seem to have been drinking from the stream since he was quite far from the edge of it. He was simply standing there. It was as if he was waiting to be noticed — not scared and more than curious — interested, I think.

"Look at you, you beautiful boy," Bliss said. "You came to see us, didn't you? You need a friend? I see you."

The buck didn't move.

"Stay still, okay, Vi?" Bliss said. Then he took a slow, careful step towards the deer.

"Hey Speckles, you want to be my deer? Like my pet? You can stay out here in the woods, but come say hi now and then. Check in with me and Vi here, let us know you're doing okay. What do you think?"

The buck remained motionless.

Bliss took another step and snapped a twig. The deer's thigh muscles tensed, but he refused to dart away. Bliss kept moving ahead until he was within a few feet of the deer.

"Bliss, stop," I whispered. "You're getting too close."

Mom had warned us again and again that wild animals were just that: wild. They were not to be chased or worse, touched. Any animal that seemed friendly probably had rabies, Mom always said — frothy mouth or not, that was one of the signs. But Bliss fed chickadees and chipmunks and little red squirrels from his hands in the winter. He said hello to every animal we ever saw in the forest, as if they understood. And he once calmly untangled a frantic jackrabbit caught in a friend's outdoor hockey net.

Bliss moved ahead once more. "Hi, Speckles," he said, just louder than a whisper.

He was within an arm's length of the deer. Speckles stared at Bliss, head slightly tilted. I'd never believe it if I wasn't seeing it happen, but Speckles seemed to want the friendly contact. I wondered then if he might be lonely. Could the other deer not like the looks of him? Could Speckles be left out, an outcast? Could he be aware there was something different about him and be feeling sad?

"Would you like that, buddy? You and me?" Bliss asked. He ever so slowly reached out and touched the side of Speckles's face.

A few seconds passed. Five, ten?

Then in one fluid twist and jump Speckles leapt away and was gone.

Bliss turned to me. His expression was pure joy, peace — happiness.

At home, Bliss and I pulled out our *Encyclopædia Britannica*s. We learned that Speckles was a piebald deer. That was why he was both brown and white — a genetic disagreement. A large section of his fur was missing the proper colouring, just not all of it. His eyes weren't pink, but the typical dark brown. Piebald deer aren't as rare as albinos, but they occur in less than one per cent of the deer population. Even people who spend a lot of time in the woods may go their whole life without seeing one. Bliss and I bragged to Mom and Dad but left out the part about Bliss touching the deer's face. I drew a picture of Speckles and gave it to Bliss. He hung it on his bedroom wall above his dresser.

When I think back on that day now, what I remember most is how Bliss spoke to Speckles and asked to claim him without a moment's hesitation. It was as if Bliss meeting and befriending Speckles was meant to be — an inevitable progress of events. Could I believe that Speckles sought Bliss out? That the deer sensed something in Bliss and was drawn to him? Maybe.

Bliss didn't just touch Speckles; Speckles touched Bliss. He extended his hand and then Speckles leaned his head into it. An agreement? A bond. And Bliss did see Speckles in the woods after that, again and again.

I haven't seen Speckles in what seems like forever — at least since late last fall. I'm so glad Foster mentioned him. Something else Bliss and I learned from the encyclopedia was that due to "environmental hazards" many deer only survive five years. But if they can avoid dangers like hunters and the highway, there's a chance they can live to be eleven or twelve. That still doesn't sound like much. We couldn't tell how old Speckles was when we first saw him, but he wasn't a fawn; he looked fully grown. So Speckles has got to be getting up there in years. At least he should have learned by now to stay away from the highway, to avoid ending up in the boneyard. And most hunters are superstitious enough to believe that it's bad luck to shoot a piebald deer.

4

There was a time when Bliss and I didn't think the boneyard existed.
When we first moved to Riverbend from the booming metropolis
of Fredericton (population 42,000), we were ridiculously considered
city kids and often had our gullibility tested. We were told that in
the summer there were mosquitoes as big as bees. Snakes hid under
every rock. There were sea monsters in the river that had come from
the ocean once they heard there was a drowned town to live in. And
there was a ghost herd, a hundred spirit deer and moose, that came
from a place called the boneyard, and haunted the woods, and even
sometimes ran out to the highway in front of cars at night. That story
was always the most detailed, so it seemed obvious that everyone was
trying way too hard to trick us. Of the many tall tales we were told, the
reality of a place called the boneyard seemed the least possible of all.

The third summer The Purple Barn was open, when I was nine and
Bliss was ten, my parents let us play unattended for whole afternoons
in the meadow behind the store. We were even allowed to play at the
forest's edge near the stream — as long as we were together, which we
always were — because it was shallow and harmless. We folded up
newspapers and made them into boats. We'd see whose would float the
longest before it got bogged down, soggy, and sank. My father gave us
a few pennies each day, which we'd toss and try to land on rocks. We'd

wade in and get them again and again. Then we'd flip them in one final time to make a wish. Bliss and I could keep ourselves entertained for hours, but of course we became more and more aware that the whole forest was right there — waiting for us to explore.

We didn't go far at first, not beyond where we could hear Mom call for us from the back door of the barn, but it gave us a whole new playground. We found a fallen log that we walked like a plank. There was a tree with a low straight branch that we could dangle and swing from. We gathered pine cones and tossed and batted them with twigs. We often saw rabbits, and at a distance one day we saw a doe and a sweet spotted fawn. There were red squirrels and chipmunks, and it always seemed that crows were flying over. They'd perch at the edge of the meadow, caw and call out as if announcing something, then fly along atop the trees.

On the last Saturday The Purple Barn was open for the season, almost at the end of October, we decided to go far deeper into the forest — way beyond the few hundred feet of woods where we usually stayed. It was Bliss's idea, but he didn't have to say much to convince me. We'd talked that whole month about the woods and the idea that there had to be spots in there no other person had ever — ever — walked on. The appeal of that was tremendous: to set our feet on a piece of the Earth that had never been touched before in the history of the world. If there were spots like that left anywhere, then surely they were in these woods in Hawkshaw, New Brunswick, Canada. Plus we loved the little bit of the forest we knew, so how could seeing and knowing more of it not be even better?

It was a warm, sunny fall day. Mom sent us out to play as soon as the store opened. We raced across the meadow and didn't turn back. We followed the stream in, staying right at its edge. We knew enough not to get lost and wreck everything. We walked over dead leaves, raised tree roots and spongy dark green moss for almost an hour before I started to doubt what we were doing and I told Bliss I thought we should head back.

"If we leave now we can go in for our snack, and Mom and Dad won't even know we were out here," I said.

He stopped and looked around. I knew when he sat down to rest he was about to agree. As much as we had wanted to go into the woods, we'd had our fun and we were tired of walking. We didn't have an end point in mind and we were already further back than we'd ever been before. Neither of us wanted to get into trouble. But then a crow landed on the top of a nearby tree and cawed out a loud message. More caws came in response, from deeper in the forest.

Bliss and I had always talked about the crows flying around the forest's edge, and we figured there was a group of nests somewhere in the woods. A rookery, Dad called it. We would often hear them cawing in the distance, but now we seemed so close to the source of the sound.

Bliss looked up at the crow then back down to me. We liked to pretend we could read each other's mind — and we really sometimes could. He stared intensely at me the way we did when we were trying to beam each other silent messages.

"Those crow nests have gotta be real close," he said. "And we're already up here."

I nodded.

"Roger, Roy Rogers?" he asked.

"Yeah," I agreed.

"Let's go, real quick, and then we'll just —" Bliss started.

"— run back real fast after," I finished.

"Okay, right now then, and let's scuff our feet in the leaves so we can see our trail," he said.

We followed the sound of the cawing. The woods were denser there with spruces and firs, poplars, cedars and a few giant pines. The underbrush was thick and we sometimes had to swat a branch out of the way, step on and squish some ferns, but we were still able to move quickly.

It wasn't long until we found the first bone.

It was half-hidden in the leaves. I almost stepped on it, but Bliss grabbed the bone and brushed it off.

"Check it out," Bliss said. He held it in front of him and turned it over in his hands.

The bone was long and off-white, smooth, old looking, the exact type of bone a cave girl would wear in her hair. He handed it to me. It was lighter than I expected.

I was jealous Bliss had picked it up first, but we started walking again and I found one too. It was nearly as long as my arm, sleek and weathered. We hit the bones together then, as if making a toast.

We thought they were probably hundreds of years old. They were unexpected prizes, perfectly timed to the season. With Halloween coming, we started scheming about building a cool skeleton decoration. Bliss said we could get Dad's drill, and I was talking about stringing the bones with white yarn. Maybe, if it turned out nice, we could put it right on the front door of the house. (Our assumption that Mom would ever allow such a thing to dangle proudly at the entry to our home is proof of how naive we were.) Bliss found two more bones. One was curved like the letter C, like a rib.

The cawing grew louder.

I began to smell something. It was subtle at first. Garbage? Manure? Rotten potatoes? I didn't recognize it, but with each step we took the smell became stronger. Sour milk. Dried blood. Spoiled meat. We walked up a little rise and came to a clearing in the trees. The sound of the crows was directly above us. The cawing was intense and constant, seemingly urgent.

We stopped at the edge of a pit.

Below were deer carcasses. Piles of them. Tossed and twisted and splayed. Some were almost whole, but many were in pieces, sprawled, decomposing, pecked at and scavenged. One body had an exposed throat, the flesh gashed and ripped, and a sunken dull, jelly-like eye. Beside it was a detached leg with blood-crusted fur above its cloven hoof.

"Violet, don't! Vi!" Bliss yelled and lunged for me. "Don't look! Wait, stop!"

But he was too late.

I already knew: the boneyard.

As his hands went around my waist to pull me back, I threw up onto the leaves.

Bliss swivelled me around. Then we ran.

We went as fast as we could, stopping only to catch our breath. We slipped and splashed along the edge of the stream. We ran and ran, paying no attention to the underbrush and low branches that scraped and sprang against our legs. It seemed to take forever until we reached the edge of the forest, raced across the meadow, and went into The Purple Barn.

Mom was at the brochure rack, sorting what was left from the season.

"Goodness, you're both out of breath," she said. "It's probably time to take a break from running around. Why don't you go have your snack in the storage room? I'll get you each a pop."

She set down the brochures. Dad was reading the newspaper behind the counter. He didn't acknowledge us. I don't remember if there were any customers in the store. Bliss and I sat at the table in the storage room. I couldn't eat. Then Mom was back and wanted us to help count the inventory in the craft section.

After supper, Bliss came to my room. I was trying to read a Trixie Belden book, but I couldn't really get into the story. Bliss sat on the chair at my desk and I stayed on the bed.

"It's real," he said. "I never believed it, but the boneyard's real."
I nodded.

"I wish you hadn't seen it, Vi," he said. "I wish I'd been able to grab you a little quicker."

I nodded again. "Yeah, it's okay though. It's not your fault."

"The deer weren't even buried," he said. "None of them. Even back when everybody told us the stories and I only imagined it as a made-up place, I thought they'd be buried. I mean, not like in a cemetery, but at least not just dumped like garbage. Some of them weren't even —," his voice trailed off.

"I know." I looked down at the bed. I tried so hard not to see it again, but the image of the tossed and rotting carcasses was like a poster taped on the front of my brain.

"We're never going back," Bliss said.

"No way," I said. I couldn't swallow the sob. I was nine years old and I had just seen more deer dead than I'd ever seen alive. I wiped my eyes.

"But we can't let it wreck the whole forest for us," Bliss said. "It's only one bad piece of a whole big good thing. And it's really far away. And we're never going back there."

"It might be pretty hard not to think about," I said. I looked back up at him.

"I know. But we have to forget it. It doesn't make any of the nice parts of the woods not nice anymore. And it's always better to think about happy stuff anyway. Okay?"

"Okay," I said.

"Okay," Bliss repeated. And he pushed the boneyard back in his mind. Tried to bury it himself. For as long as he could.

5

When I return from Foster's, I take Dean to the house with me. I let him drive the truck so I can hold Pepper Shaker, the shop's black cat. He was sleeping in his favourite spot, a little worn burgundy needlepoint footstool that never sells — perhaps because it's covered with cat hair, or perhaps because Pepper Shaker is always on it, his tail strategically curled over the price tag. He's an indoor cat now. We used to let him out in the back field to go mousing, but his preference for killing colourful birds instead never went over well with the tourists. Pepper Shaker couldn't be happy with a little brown sparrow; his tastes ran more exotic, to cardinals, goldfinches and rarely seen Baltimore orioles. No one wants to see a cat with beautiful red feathers in its mouth. Everyone is always more upset when it's something beautiful that dies.

Along with the population printed on the "Welcome to Riverbend" sign is the slogan "We've been planning on you," which is a lame inside joke that I'm sure few visitors to the place understand. Riverbend was set up by the government after the permanent flood, as an option (peace offering is what Dad says) for people who lost their homes but wanted to stay in the area — on dry land. It's a planned town. Lots of locals did move in along with some new arrivals like us. Mom says that even though our family doesn't have the same history or connection to the area, the way that everyone started fresh in town together meant we were never really treated like outsiders.

Riverbend has nine streets total — eight of them criss-cross in the middle and then a long road that follows the bend of the river loops around the outside. The homes and schools and churches and even a little mall are all neatly arranged. There's no sprawl. It really is small, tiny even. Not only does everyone know everyone, but in the course of an evening you could saunter by all their houses. That doesn't mean that what happens here isn't a big deal though; it's as if there's a magnification factor to make up for the size of the place. Little news becomes big news and big news becomes huge breaking news. If anything even remotely interesting occurs — from someone finding a double-yolked egg to someone falling off a ladder — word will spread. You can plan on that.

Our house is two storeys, wide and white, along the road that circles the outside of town. It has giant windows that Dad had made special order, so one side is almost a wall of glass with a view of the water. The house is built into a slight hill, and you can walk right out the basement patio door at ground level and head down to the river.

The inside is nice, but nothing showy or museum-like even though we have plenty of antiques. We have modern furniture too — realistically sized couches that are actually comfortable. We have a big kitchen and living room that often serve as the meeting place for almost every women's group and organization in Riverbend. My mother, Anne, is a Lioness, a volunteer at the public library, a member of the ladies' bridge club and is the secretary for the Riverbend Community Days committee. Plus she always volunteered and helped in the school when I was younger. Jill used to call her the Queen of

Riverbend. My mother used to be exactly who Jill wanted to be when she grew up.

I carry Pepper Shaker inside and let him loose in the kitchen. He starts sniffing the legs of the stools at the counter. He lives with us in the house all winter, but I wonder what he thinks being here this time of year.

Dean helps me open all the windows. I water the plants. I look in the garage to make sure nothing is any different from the way my parents left it.

Then Dean and I go down to the dock. It's only about eight feet long, made of lumber Dad got with an estate a few years ago. We take off our shoes and sit at the very end to let our legs dangle into the water. The sunlight makes golden squiggles along the ripples of the river, raising and lowering on the teeniest waves. Someone has a sailboat way upstream, but around here not a lot of people go out on the water. Maybe it's because the old town is under there. In the same way you don't walk over a grave, maybe people can't bring themselves to float above the dead town. Too many ghosts. It seems this whole area is filled with some type of ghost.

We sit in silence. There's a slight breeze so I tuck my hair behind my ears. Dean kicks his feet and splashes my ankles. I splash back.

"You should've taken me out to see Foster with you," Dean finally says.

I shake my head slightly. "He's fine. But thanks."

"You know your dad's about the only person around here who'll have anything to do with him. And I don't buy the stupid rumours that he eats the rotten roadkill from the boneyard and it makes him crazy, but —"

"Oh, is that the latest?" I interrupt.

Dean splashes me enough that water sprays up on my face. "I know he's probably harmless, but his place is a long way back there. And it's not like we can phone him to see that you got there safe. That's all."

I shrug.

"Fair enough," I say.

I don't mind that Dean worries about me — as long as it's only a little bit.

When Dean says we should probably get back to the store I know he's right. Inside the house we start closing windows, and Pepper Shaker looks annoyed when the noise of the sliding panes wakes him. He'd been curled into a black ball on the couch, like an antique bear-fur muff we have at the store.

The phone rings and although I'm sure it's Quinny telling us to hurry along, I answer.

"Hello, Violet."

"Dad, it's you."

"Quinny said you were at the house. I hope you're being at least decent to that old bird."

"Maybe. So anything yet?"

Dean looks at me, waiting for the answer.

"No, nothing yet," Dad says. A pause. I shake my head at Dean, and he goes back to closing windows.

"We keep showing his picture at every gas station and restaurant, but he was probably hitchhiking. For all we know he could've caught a ride right past them. We're —," he pauses and I can hear Mom say something to him.

"But we're just getting started," Dad says. "We're really just getting started. We're barely into Quebec so far, not even to Rivière-du-Loup yet." He clears his throat. I wait, except I know that's all he's going to say on the subject. Instead he asks about my trip to see Foster, tells me to spend what I need to get the estate. He asks about the campsite and the house and Dean and Jill.

I talk to Mom for a few minutes too. She says she's been having lots of opportunities to speak French, which is a good thing, right? She'll be all practiced-up for the Quebec tourists who come in the store later in the summer. "Bonjour, est-ce que je peux vous aider?" Mom says. She's talking in the well-rehearsed cheerful tone she uses for our customers, and has been since she took the phone from Dad. "Oui, voilà la salle de bains," she says and laughs. I'm sure she's trying to sound upbeat for my benefit, but knowing that it's fake makes it hard to listen to.

Dean and I arrive at The Purple Barn about twenty minutes before the posted closing time, but the lot is still full. We get hundreds of people every day. Dad's counted a few times over the years. He figured on our busiest days we could have a thousand people, if we added in every child and baby. That's the equivalent of the whole town of Riverbend passing through the store — driving down the highway, here and gone. Then the next day, more people. And we stay in the one spot and watch them go.

I tell Quinny and Elizabeth it's okay if they leave and that Dean and I will close up. We never kick customers out of the store, my father absolutely forbids it — we are Maritimers, we are friendly — but as Dean starts to carry in items from the display outside, people clue in. I work the cash. I sell a pair of brass candlesticks, a book and a souvenir felt pennant, a CNR railway lantern with a red glass globe, a bottle of local maple syrup and a macramé owl perched on a piece of Saint John River driftwood.

Dean goes home and I take a final look around the store to be sure we haven't missed anyone. Pepper Shaker rubs against my leg. Someone bought his little footstool while we were gone. Poor kitty. I find an old galvanized washtub and spread two burlap flour bags across the bottom of it. I carry it to the spot where the footstool had been and put Pepper Shaker inside. He hops right out and meows a long scratchy yowl.

"I know, Shakes." I pick him up and put him back in, then scratch between his ears until he lowers his bum into a sitting position. As soon as I stop the scratching he hops back out again and walks away meowing. I'll wait and see what he's chosen for himself tomorrow.

Jill volunteered us to help Dwayne at Seven Birches. It's going to be Christmas in July. Dwayne overheard a tourist talking about a campground in Michigan celebrating it so he decided to try it here. Lots of campers stay for the whole season at Seven Birches, and he likes to keep them entertained.

There's already a big snowman made of quilt batting up on the roof of The Snack Shack. It's shifted a bit sideways and has buckled in the middle under the weight of its spray-painted white basketball head. It looks like it's melting in the sun. There's a shiny silver garland across the top of the takeout window and a pair of Santa and Mrs. Claus salt and pepper shakers sitting on the shelf between the bottles of ketchup and mustard. The cedar trees on each side of the step are wound with multicoloured lights, and it's our job to take the remaining fifteen strands and put them up wherever we choose. We line the top of the fence around the whole pool. We trim the clump of spruce trees in front of the washrooms. We clip the last string to the New Brunswick flag, raise it, then wrap the lights around the pole.

Dwayne shows up for the Christmas Carol campfire singalong in a complete Santa suit and hat, except he's wearing sandals instead of boots. He's sweating and his face is the same colour as his costume. There are three green bows stuck to the front of his guitar and a gold garland wound along the strap. Families are gathered around the campfire on the low log benches and some people are behind them on lawn chairs or blankets. Jill and I carried over the two rocking chairs from the porch of our cottage. Dwayne starts strumming and leads everyone in "Rudolph the Red-Nosed Reindeer," "Deck the Halls" and then "Jingle Bells." I think almost everyone staying at Seven Birches is here.

Dwayne's wife arrives with a bag of marshmallows for the snowball roast. She has sticks and generously shoves five marshmallows on each one before handing them off to the children. Santa sings "It's a Marshmallow World." A car drives fast into the campsite on the gravel road behind us. It's a white Ford Mustang with a wide blue stripe and a Quebec licence plate. We're a big crowd, singing loudly, being led by a man in a Santa suit, and yet the driver of the car seems completely unaware, windows down, radio blaring. Almost everyone turns around to look for the source of the noise. As the car approaches I can see that the driver is my neighbour from the cabin next door. But then, as if he suddenly clues in, he turns his radio off. He slows the car down to a crawl as he pulls in the roadway that leads to the cabins. I watch as he parks and, without glancing back, heads in. I wonder what his deal is.

The singalong continues until there's a rumble of thunder in the distance. I can tell Dwayne's just as happy to wrap it up anyway. He wishes everyone a Merry Christmas, pulls off his Santa hat and wipes the sweat from his face with it. Jill and I take our rocking chairs back to the porch. The sun isn't quite set, but the storm clouds have made the sky instantly dark.

Jill goes to The Snack Shack to call Johnny from the pay phone.

I take a seat in one of the rocking chairs. The lightning starts and the thunder gets louder. Then the rain comes in a downpour. My legs get wet from the splashing drops landing on the porch edge. The heavy rain pounds the surface of the river, making the water look like it has come to a furious boil. But the storm passes quickly; it doesn't even last long enough to cool the temperature much.

Jill comes back and goes in for the night.

There's a final bright flash of heat lightning right above the river that is so intense it makes me wonder if it could illuminate the drowned town. If you were out on the water and looking down in exactly the right place, would it glow? For those few electric seconds would the town seem to be brought back to life? Like a New Brunswick Atlantis? But then I wonder if I closed all the windows over at the house or did I miss one and did rain get in? I think of Dad calling. And my parents looking. Asking people what they remember, or if they remember. Does he look familiar? Have you seen him? His name is Bliss. Bliss Davis. A weight inside me settles low. It feels like a rock sinks to the bottom of my stomach and stays there in the dark like the town in the river.

I lie in bed and think of the Christmas I was ten. Mom's mother, Gram, was still alive then and had stayed overnight. After we opened our presents, Gram helped Mom get the big dinner ready while Bliss and I played with our new toys. I got a Barbie and Skipper and lots of outfits for them, so I stayed in the room with the Christmas tree and had a fashion show. I was surprised Bliss didn't play with his new car-racing track, but when he went to his room, I figured it was to read one of his books.

When dinner was almost ready, I went to find him. He was lying on his bed, staring at the ceiling. I could tell he'd been crying. I sat beside him on the edge of the bed.

"Are you okay?"

He shook his head.

"Why were you crying?"

He shook his head again. He didn't move otherwise and didn't look at me.

"I'm not sure," he finally said.

I didn't think people could be sad without a reason. Plus it was Christmas — the happiest day of the year. I thought he just didn't want to tell me why.

"What do you mean? You really don't know?"

"I don't. I really don't. It just, I — I feel sad, like something sad happened. I don't know — I just — maybe it's something I should have felt bad about before, but forgot to? I —" He stopped and took in a deep breath. "I just feel sad, and I think I was trying to figure out why, like maybe remember something. Do you remember when January ran away?" January was a white cat we had before Pepper Shaker.

"You're thinking about January?"

"What if I should have looked for her more? I think maybe I should have."

"No," I said, shaking my head. "No. And that was such a long time ago." I was starting to feel scared. Bliss turned away from me, rolled over to face the wall. "Are you sure you didn't hurt yourself?"

I reached over to feel his forehead the way Mom did when she thought we might be sick. He felt normal. I smoothed his hair.

"Bliss, what is it really? Tell me."

"Violet," he whispered, "Vi."

He flipped back over and sat up. "I really think I might feel bad because of the boneyard."

It was the first time he'd mentioned the boneyard since we'd been there more than a year ago. We'd had a whole summer of fun playing in the woods again — in the good, happy parts we loved — and the boneyard had become a distant memory for me. I thought it had for Bliss too.

"The boneyard? I don't understand. Why?"

He shook his head and a tear ran down his face. "I don't know for sure, but Violet — what if the ghosts don't come from the boneyard because they're mad, what if they come because they're sad? What if they're sad that people have forgotten about them and left them there? I didn't believe it was even real. I should have believed. And they weren't buried, Vi. I should have done something. I could have—"

A knock on the bedroom door. Gram opened it and stepped in. The smile on her face disappeared.

"Are you hurt, Bliss?" she asked. Her voice was stern.

He shook his head. He wiped his cheeks and ran his fingers across his eyelashes.

"Well I certainly hope those aren't ungrateful tears. I can't imagine that even children as spoiled as you could be disappointed with that mountain of gifts your parents gave you. You know when I was young I would only ever get a few barley treats and maybe a book, and I was the happiest girl in the Junction.

"You wash your face now Bliss, and then both of you come set the table. It's Christmas and your parents will not be seeing any sulking on Christmas."

"Gram," I said, "Bliss isn't —"

She cut me off. "Violet, nothing more. Not another word of this. Why don't you go put a nice dress on?"

I looked at Bliss.

Gram stood by the door, insistent, waiting, until I left.

When we all sat down to dinner, Bliss was quiet. He had some potatoes and gravy but no turkey and took only one small scoop of the broccoli casserole Mom made especially for him. I smiled at him across the table, but he stared straight ahead. I knew he was still thinking about the boneyard. So I started telling Gram about Speckles. It was the only way I could figure to move Bliss's mind from the bad to the good of the forest. Bliss had met Speckles just that past spring, and the encounter seemed to fill the forest with a type of magic again.

I went on about how smart Speckles was, saying how I was sure he remembered us the second time we saw him and then, considering that Gram's house always smelled like Pine-Sol and Javex, I mentioned how clean he kept his gorgeous white fur.

When Gram said, "My goodness, and can this fantastical deer fly too?" I ignored her mocking tone and launched into speculation of how wonderful Speckles would be as one of Santa's reindeer.

Bliss didn't say much as we ate, or for the rest of the day. He lost when we played Boggle, which rarely happened. He had even fewer points than Dad who plays without his reading glasses and can't tell the difference between an *O*, *C*, *D*, *Q* or *G*. Bliss agreed to only two hands of rummy and then said he was going to bed early. Mom seemed concerned, but Bliss claimed he hadn't slept well and was tired.

"Oh to be young and to lose sleep with that much anticipation for Christmas morning again," Mom said and shook her head.

Bliss slept in until noon on Boxing Day. Then once he woke, he read most of the afternoon. But there were no more tears, and he didn't try to talk to me about the boneyard again.

I didn't bring it up with Bliss after that because I thought he might be embarrassed. It was so odd, it was like the whole incident had come out of nowhere — like a defective Christmas miracle. I thought of what Bliss had said over and over, trying to figure it out. It was like his brain made a mistake and gave him the wrong emotion on a happy day. Sure, you could feel bad about events after they happened, or think about them much later and still have some of the same feelings. I know when I accidentally hit a boy in the face with a baseball, I was compelled to apologize all over again when I saw that he still had a faint bruise the next week. But that was different from Bliss's experience because I knew why I felt bad. Cause and effect; perfectly logical. With Bliss it was as if he had the effect first, the feeling, and then he couldn't figure out the cause. Except you can't have an emotion without a reason, right?

So Bliss thought he must have just forgotten why he felt sad. Then, when he desperately dug around in his brain, he thought it might have something to do with the boneyard. Our trip there and seeing all those dead deer at once had been the worst thing he had experienced in his short life up to that point. Who knows why it happened. Could he have eaten something weird? Drank Dad's rum-infused eggnog instead of our plain kind? Breathed in fumes while he slept? (At the time, these didn't seem like such far-fetched possibilities for an incident so strange it surely had to be a one-time fluke.)

I came to the conclusion that it was best if I forgot about the whole thing. I didn't have to worry about Bliss. There was no way it could happen again.

I wake in the night. The cottage feels like it's the temperature of a little kid's fever. Even in just my T-shirt and underwear, with the one sheet I had over me in a tangled knot at my feet, I'm roasting. I go to the window and see if I can open it any wider. Dwayne has left all the Christmas lights on, twinkling in the night. I pull my hair up into a ponytail before I lie back on the bed.

I flip my pillow. I try a few different positions but I can't fall asleep. I pull on some shorts, grab a cold bottle of Sprite from the fridge and slip out the door. (Jill could sleep through an asteroid landing on the cottage, so she doesn't even shift in her bed.) There's a light on at our neighbour's place. Maybe he's having trouble sleeping too. I walk along the road that winds between the campsites. It's hard to see the licence plates in the dark, but I do notice a long camper from Connecticut. A van from PEI. The sound of the rocks crunching under my sandals is loud in the night and almost seems to echo subtly over the river. The highway is quiet, so it must be long past midnight, when a lot of the truckers pull off to rest.

I go back to the porch. I sit on a rocker at first but then I shove the pop bottle in the back pocket of my shorts, hop onto the porch railing, and pull myself onto the roof. I sit on the peak, which is slightly damp from the rain earlier. The view is really good up here. Behind me, across the river, is the tiny grid of streetlights of Riverbend, and to my left are the Christmas lights, colourful little dots sparkling. But off to the right and along the highway towards The Purple Barn, it's dark. The yellow centre line gradually disappears into the shadows. Everything in the distance is hidden behind a solid black wall.

Then, from the darkness, perhaps two hundred feet away, comes something white. And bright?

A buck. It's huge and it seems to shine as if it has an internal source of light.

In the time it took me to blink, it moved from the cover of night onto the shoulder of the highway. Its antlers, at least ten points on each side, are shining too, glistening like they are made of glass. I gasp and it feels as if every bit of moisture in my mouth dries out. I can't take my eyes off the deer. It walks to the centre of the road and stops, bows its head. I stand and inch carefully down the steep pitch of the roof to see it better. I hear a vehicle, something big like a transport, in the distance. I see the faintest hint of headlights behind the animal, but the buck isn't moving. Can't it sense the vehicle coming? I want to yell to it. Move. Move! But it is so far away.

I take another step, and my sandal slips out from under me. Within seconds I land first on the very edge of the roof then fall to the hard ground below. I get up as fast as I can. My shorts are soaked with pop, my right thigh is throbbing, and I think I cut my right hand on the broken bottle. I run around the front of the cottage, hop on the porch rail and pull myself back onto the roof. I hear the truck go by — no horn, no brakes, no tires screeching, no thud. I stand on the peak and stare at the highway. The beautiful white buck is gone.

Deer usually get killed on the highway because they move too fast. Moose are hit because they move too slow. Deer rush, leap and land on hoods, smash into windshields. They seem to come from nowhere. In three bounds they can go from the forest edge to the shoulder to the yellow centre line. And there is often more than one. My parents warned Bliss and me again and again that if we ever saw a deer to watch for another — a pair, a group, a herd. A son, a daughter, family, friends.

Moose just stand there. Or walk slowly, seemingly like *I-was-here-first*, without a care. They are the biggest creatures we have in the province, probably the biggest animal you've ever seen. They are so tall that the headlights of a car can't even show all of them. A moose gets hit in the ankles or knees by a car, has its legs taken out from under it, and it buckles, collapses and crushes the car roof. People often don't survive a collision with a moose. But moose are rare around here. The moose carcasses in the boneyard have been brought in from upriver, where there are bogs and marshes near the highway.

I wash my hands and cover my cut. It takes four Band-Aids. I'm going to have a big bruise on my thigh. I go back to bed but I'm even more awake than before.

What was that? That deer. The buck.

Speckles?

Yes. Of course it was Speckles. He was far away and the moonlight shining on his fur made him appear to glow pure white.

And there was no sound; he wasn't hit or hurt. He ran back to the forest. Safe again.

As a child, I always figured God was so smart and all-knowing that even in the beginning He knew one day there would be cars and trucks with headlights that would drive along on roads which animals needed to cross sometimes. It was why He made their eyes glow and flash when they reflected the light. It gave the animals a chance to be seen at night; it was their little built-in protection, however small. Now that God seems hardly likely, and I doubt any such divine invention just as much as divine intervention, I wonder if it's a genetic adaptation that evolved as man took over nature. Or if, perhaps, it's a lucky coincidence.

I'm glad Foster saw Speckles, and I have to think that I'm glad I finally saw him again too. Sometimes Foster calls Speckles the hart, or Bliss's hart, which is another name for a male deer. But I don't. I can't. I know Speckles only as a buck. It's corny, but there's something I thought of years ago that I can't forget.

Hart sounds the same as *heart*. And hearts can be broken.

6

I stay at the store counter until noon, carefully perched on the stool. It doesn't hurt when I walk, but sitting on the bruise makes my whole thigh feel sore. Dean noticed the Band-Aids on my hand first thing this morning. I shrugged it off. I know he'll ask me about it again later, and I haven't quite decided what to say. I'd rather not think about last night at all.

I'm going to stretch my legs and dust for a bit before lunch. Usually I would tease Pepper Shaker with the feather duster and he'd swat and jump, but I think he's still annoyed with me. He was nowhere near his makeshift bed of the washtub and flour bags when I came in, and there was no cat-hair evidence that he'd even given it a test drive. Last time I saw him he was asleep in a wooden orange crate but his tail was flicking around as if he was having nightmares.

"Violet," a man says behind me. It's Quinny's husband, George. He's a retired math teacher and still wears the short-sleeved dress shirts he used to wear to school. Today his shirt is a pale yellow, freshly pressed with the collar just so. His grey hair is parted on the side and slicked back. He has an even tan and brown eyes. He looks a bit younger than Quinny. There's a new quilt draped over his arm.

I nod at it.

"You expecting to take a chill?"

He laughs and lifts the quilt. "Alvina forgot it in the car this morning when I dropped her off. Thought I'd bring it over once I noticed. But I wanted to show it to you first before she hangs it."

He holds it up in front of him. It's a small quilt, dangling from his chin to his knees. A baby quilt, I guess, for a girl, done in a combination of white and a pretty dainty lilac floral print. Each block has a simple building on it, made of a rectangle with a long triangle roof and a white square for a door. There are six of them. Little fabric purple barns.

"It's sweet," I say. "Some girl will be lucky to have it."

George folds the quilt and passes it to me.

"So what are you up to today?" I ask as I walk with him to the front door of the barn. Quinny works so much that he must spend a lot of time hanging out by himself.

"Oh, garden, groceries, got to run up to Woodstock for a minute. I like staying busy." He smiles as if he really is looking forward to it all.

I say goodbye to him and as I turn to head back to Quinny, who's behind the counter, she quickly averts her eyes.

After lunch, Dad's dealer friend Joey shows up to buy some things from The Room. He takes a complete flow blue dinnerware set, a matched pair of ebonized side tables, a set of twelve matching pressed-back chairs, two plant stands and a whole box of smaller items. Everything comes to almost seven hundred dollars, but he'll be able to sell it all again at his store in Ontario for plenty more. It's how the antiques business works. Lots of pieces pass through dealer after dealer, each person buying then selling them, making a bit of profit, before they are finally sold to a collector. Dad claims that if dealers ever stopped buying from each other, the whole antiques marketplace would collapse.

I give the cash to Quinny. She's used to me handing over big amounts from dealers, so she simply tucks it away in the bottom of the register. I tell her I'm leaving early and I'm almost to the front door before she calls me back.

"We've heard again from the woman with the estate to sell. It's just a cottage, down at Pine Lake, so I doubt you'll need Mr. Kensey to go with you. It's likely quite manageable, so I think it would be best if I simply went along."

"When did she call?"

"While you were in your vault. I didn't want to disturb your business, so I just made the arrangements," Quinny says.

"When does she want me to go?"

"She suggested next Saturday, and I said we would gladly come then."

We. Quinny has never been to an estate nor ever asked to go to one. She's also never before worried about calling me from *the vault* (The Room) since every time the door opens she gets to peek inside. But I'm sure Dad will call again soon enough and straighten her out. I have other things to think about for now.

I want to talk to Dean before I leave. He's outside washing all the little windows lined along the front of the barn. He takes a break, and rather than go back to the woods, we sit on the picnic table at the side of the parking lot.

"So are you going to tell me what happened?" He lifts my hand.

"I told you this morning. I broke some glass," I say.

"Right. But I missed the how part. That's not just a nick."

I shrug. "You wouldn't believe me if I told you."

"Try me."

I wait. Consider. Smile. "Well there was this ghost deer —"

"Jesus! Where?" Dean shouts and looks around frantically. He catapults himself backwards and hides low behind the picnic table.

I flinch; I can't help myself. A chill comes over me and the sweat on the back of my neck turns clammy.

Dean laughs. "Whoa, Vi! Holy liftin'! I'm kidding," he says. "You should see the look on your face." Then he stands again and puts a hand on my shoulder. "Hey," he says. "Sorry. Really."

"You're evil," I say and breathe in quickly. I give him a little shove. Smile and shake my head. A customer in the parking lot who witnessed the scene starts walking again to the door.

"You're jumpy," he says.

"Yeah, maybe," I admit. "But don't worry about the hand. It's nothing. As I said: trip, break glass, cut hand, end of story."

"Yeah, that's cool. But really Vi, you seem pretty edgy. You doing okay?"

A crow flies and lands on the corner of the barn roof, caws at us, then continues on to the forest, presumably back to the boneyard. I watch it go.

"Don't worry about me," I say. "And anyway, remember how I told you that Jill's keeping me busy? Her big plan: Special Mission Violet's Fun Summer. Well, that's what I wanted to tell you. I'm leaving now, going down to the Landing."

"You having supper there?"

"No, a wedding. Jill got me a job as extra help with the reception."

"You wearing the big get-up?"

"I am."

"Well it's pretty damn painful I don't get to see your good-looking self in that old outfit."

"You'll live."

"I suppose. Me and Johnny and Barkley are going fishing for an hour or so tonight, then I'm going out to visit my uncle." He lifts my hand and kisses it on the Band-Aids. "Have fun, Vi. Just promise me you won't trip on your skirt and break anything, or spill on the bride."

"I'll try my best," I say.

I get in the truck, roll both windows all the way down, and wait what seems like an eternity for a chance to turn out of the barn parking lot. Jill might be onto something with her plan to keep me busy, because a visit to Kings Landing will be a welcome distraction. Her boss knows my father, so it was easy for her to get me the gig. I'm sure he's confident enough with my knowledge of all things old-timey that he figures I can carry around an antique silver tray of cucumber finger sandwiches at a Victorian-themed wedding without saying anything stupid.

About three miles down the highway, I drive past what I know is the official road to the boneyard. It looks like any other logging road winding way back into the woods with deep tire tracks and branches of alder bushes encroaching on each side, just high enough to thwack a vehicle in the windshield. There's a chain across the entry with a sign that says "No Trespassing" and "Province of NB," but nothing to warn birdwatchers or hikers that the road ends in a pit of death. At least deer and moose aren't hit along the highway daily. The Undertakers don't drive a marked patrol vehicle, like an animal safety security force, up-and downriver, watching for recent kills. They are mostly responsible for things like trimming the tall brush along the sides of the roadway and mowing the lawn in the few places where there's a grass median. They take care of the flower gardens planted near overpasses and strategically weed the marigolds at the New Brunswick–Maine border so the blooming letters spelling out "Welcome" are always clear. They are responsible for emptying the garbage cans at the rest stops and scenic lookouts along the highway. They are really caretakers more than undertakers.

I've thought before that the Undertakers could very well be the ones who started the whole rumour turned to legend turned to myth of the ghost herd. Maybe they were sitting in their truck one day on a smoke break and the idea started as a joke. Then once some beer was involved and the story was repeated on a few Saturday nights, there was no turning back. They claim the woods are haunted, but the Undertakers brave them regardless. Easy as that, their boring job became a lot more intriguing.

Really, the boneyard could be forgotten and left alone to serve its gruesome purpose if it wasn't for the ghost deer. Although it could never cease to exist entirely. Unless there is some massive fence built someday to keep them out, deer can't be protected from the highway. The little Department of Transportation signs warning of deer are a bit of a joke (several along here have even been graffitied with a little man riding the jumping deer, like a cowboy on a bucking bronco). We know enough to be wary of them. I wish they knew better to be wary of us.

I take the exit to Kings Landing. The historical village was created so some of the best and oldest houses in the area could be saved when the area was flooded. Jill talks about it in her official spiel. Some houses were moved by truck; some were slid down the ice of the river in winter. Some were partially disassembled, cut into pieces, moved and then put back together on-site. The most impressive story is of an all-stone house, called the Jones House, which was moved stone by stone. It was completely taken apart, and then put back together again. You'd never know now, looking at the place. It's even built into a hill and the slope is perfect.

I turn down the staff entrance, which is a long dirt road that ends in a cluster of modern buildings, well hidden from the historic houses by an acre of trees. I go to the costume department, where four ladies make outfits for the eighty staff. Their workshop is a big rectangular room with two long tables with sewing machines right in the middle. One whole wall is a shelving unit with bolts of fabric in solid colours of slate blue, hunter green, deep burgundy and rust, as well as matching calico prints. There's an oak cabinet with dozens of little drawers and several rolls of ribbons, bags of feathers and straw hats piled on top.

"Violet, good to see you," a woman says as she approaches me. It's Elsie McKay. She lives in Riverbend too and comes in the antique store sometimes. She collects pincushion dolls, which are made with a little china doll body in the middle and a puffy stuffed fabric skirt for pins. Today she wears a little pincushion on her wrist like a bracelet.

"You're here for the wedding, right?" Elsie asks. "So how about we go with a nice burgundy? We've got a new hat that will match as well." Elsie gathers my whole outfit, including shoes, accessories, and an elastic and bobby pins for my hair. She notices the Band-Aids on my hand and gives me gloves to wear for the actual serving later.

"You can get suited up in the washroom there, and then I'll help you out with the adjustments. And be sure to wipe your eyeshadow off." There is a no makeup rule for staff. No blue eyeshadow in the 1800s means no blue eyeshadow now.

I get all ready: slip, bustle, full-length burgundy skirt, a pink calico blouse with a high neck and puffed sleeves. I have a little beige cro-cheted purse (officially called a reticule) that I put the truck keys in. I French braid my hair and tuck the end in with bobby pins. Then there's the hat. It is straw and wide-brimmed, but one whole half of it has been tacked up. It is decorated with a deep rich burgundy ribbon and a pink silk rose with three burgundy and two white feathers curling out from underneath it. I put it on and look in the mirror. I wonder, if my ancestors could see me now, if they'd think I look pretty, stylish, flashy or ridiculous. I head out for Elsie's inspection.

"I heard your parents got away," she says as she looks me over. "Goodness knows, they certainly deserve a nice vacation. My." She nods her head. "Where was it they went though, Violet? Are they down in —"

I let the reticule slip through my fingers. It lands with a thud. "Sorry," I say. I pick it up and shake it. "My keys are in there. And I should probably get going. Did you say I needed a hat pin?"

"I've got one right here," she says and picks one up off a nearby table. The thing is an absolute weapon. It's a foot long with a black ball on one end. Elsie adjusts my hat a bit then pokes the pin through the hat, my braid, and hat again.

She stands back for a final look at me. "You're beautiful, Violet," Elsie says. "You be a good girl now."

The wedding reception doesn't start for an hour and a half, so I walk to the church. A little white picket fence surrounds the whole yard. The grass is freshly cut. A stone pathway leads to a large black door, which is propped open with a big rock. Clear glass vases of wildflowers are set in each of the windows. It's a small, modest, white wooden country church, and a few bouquets will be the only decorations for the wedding ceremony. Anything modern, like streamers or balloons, are not allowed.

I go up the walkway and have a peek inside. There are a couple of tourists looking at the antique pump organ and another older man and woman are quietly chatting in one of the pews. A generous bunch of mainly daisies and brown-eyed Susans are set on a stand at the front. The hymn numbers are in place on the board. The building is hot and stuffy with the slightest smell of dry wood, something similar to the scent of old books, but much stronger. The guests will sweat.

Back outside, there's a family in the churchyard. A boy, he's maybe six or seven, says something to his mother and points at me. The mother shakes her head, but then I hear him say, "Please, come on. Do it, Mom."

She turns to face me.

"Beautiful day for your visit," I say.

"I'm sorry," she starts, "but my son wanted me to ask you something. I hope it's all right."

She glances quickly over to the little graveyard beside the church. There are ten or twelve headstones, worn and grey, each with names and dates.

"There's no one actually buried there," I say. "By any chance was that what you were wondering?"

The boy looks shocked. He must think I'm psychic.

"That's a popular question around here," I say to the woman, and she looks relieved. "The headstones are exact replicas, and all the names and dates are the same, it's just the people are buried somewhere else." The mother nods but then suddenly leaves to chase after a little girl who has run into the church. Their father, standing smoking at the far end of the graveyard, must not have noticed her go.

"So it's fake dead people?" the boy asks.

"I guess so," I say.

He grins and looks delighted, but then his face turns serious. "Do you think the ghosts get confused?" he asks. "Like about what place they're supposed to haunt. Do you think they know which one the real grave is?"

"I'm not sure," I say and shrug. "Maybe ghosts aren't even real."

"They're real!" the boy insists. "Not like Casper, he's stupid, but everybody has a cold-breath ghost that's real."

I have no idea what he's talking about, and I know from working at the barn there are some little kids you shouldn't encourage. They can turn out to be as rambling and chatty as adults with too much time to kill. But the boy's mother is still inside the church, and his father is still smoking. So, yeah, why not?

"What do you mean cold-breath ghost?"

He scrunches his eyebrows like he's suddenly suspicious of me, as if I'm not a normal, halfway intelligent person in a period costume, but have instead been dropped off here via time travel from some less-informed era of the past.

"When you can see your breath in the winter outdoors. That's some of the ghost inside you trying to sneak out early. Because ghosts are cold. I read in a book once that they give you chills if you accidentally walk through one so I figured it out."

Smart little guy.

"Good enough," I say.

"So I'm going to remember about this fake graveyard and ask sometime. I don't know anyone dead yet," he goes on. "But as soon as someone I know gets dead and they're a ghost, I'm going to remember to ask them to ask these ghosts. Do you think that sounds like a good idea?"

I nod.

"Do you know anyone dead yet?"

I shouldn't have encouraged him. I look over my shoulder. "Oh sorry, I thought I heard your mom calling for you," I say.

"But you don't even know my name."

I have to smile. I bet he drives his parents crazy. He really is cute though. He has dark brown eyes with long dark lashes and freckles.

"So what is it then?" I ask.

"James," he says.

"Well it's been nice talking to you James, but I've got to get going."

His mother is finally approaching, carrying his little sister. James says goodbye to me then runs towards them.

. . .

The wedding reception is at the Ingraham House. There are four other women besides Jill and me, as well as Mr. Lowe who usually acts as shopkeeper in the general store. He's dressed in a top hat and coat. Guests will arrive and mingle in the beautiful garden out back until they've eaten their fill of hors d'ouevres. Then we'll be done and the wedding party will go down to the King's Head Inn for a proper meal.

Jill and I are sent out early to the yard to make sure everything looks perfect — that there are no dead mice deposited by one of the barn cats onto the pathway, that there's no garbage anywhere or no bird droppings on the big brass sundial. We quickly walk through the four quadrants of the large English garden, each a beautiful square made of every colour and shape of flower, then we walk under the trellis covered in ivy and morning glory to wait for the wedding party.

The group heads towards us in a small black carriage pulled by a single brown horse. The bride and groom are sitting on a raised seat behind the driver. The bride is fair-skinned with striking black hair. She and the groom are smiling and laughing. The rest of the wedding party and guests are walking behind them, the full width of the dirt road, with the churchyard on one side and the beautiful yellow Perley house on the other. There are two little flower girls in matching purple dresses skipping along. There's so much chatter and laughter.

Jill is entranced. I'm sure she's taking notes. Jill talks about her future wedding all the time. She isn't engaged yet, but she's positive Johnny is the one. The One. He will be her husband, the father of her children. They've been together since grade nine.

Their romantic meeting took place after church one morning. Johnny had wanted to know who won the hockey game, because he had fallen asleep before it was over. Jill had heard her father and older brother talking about it in the car. The Canadiens (who Johnny loved) had scored to beat the Leafs (who Johnny loathed). And the fact that Jill was the bearer of the good news determined the course of the rest of her life. It became Jill and Johnny's history, and if all goes according to Jill's plan, the start of a story to tell their grandchildren. There are so many incidents that can start out small and don't seem like anything at the time but end up meaning so much. There are so many tiny twists in a life that you can never know the ultimate significance of.

As near as I can tell, Johnny's only future goal is to win the Demolition Derby at Riverbend Community Days in September. He has a beat-up, dented Mercury Meteor in a bay at his father's repair shop that he's painted the same purple as our barn — with orange and red flames curling around the wheel wells, then all across the hood. The flames look more like flowers growing up from the tires, but the hood is pretty good. Charles J. Davis and Son Antiques is Johnny's business sponsor, so my father gave him some of the leftover purple paint and fifty dollars to do whatever. My father's all about being a part of the community. (He was also Jill's sponsor when she won second princess in the Miss Riverbend Pageant last year.) He claims it's good for business — even if it means letting a teenager smash his car into other old beaters until they conk out, in a muddy field beside the Legion, while the crowd breathes in exhaust fumes and hopes no one's vehicle catches fire.

But I suppose there's a good chance Johnny will win. His father is the town mechanic and Johnny already knows a ton about cars. If Johnny's drinking you have to be really careful to avoid the subject or he'll start talking about articles he's read in *Hot Rod* magazine. He went for a tour of both the Bricklin parts plant in Minto and the assembly plant in Saint John a couple of years ago. You'd think he'd been to NASA the way he went on and on. The Bricklins have these crazy gull-wing doors that flap open bottom to top instead of swinging out to the sides. Johnny demonstrated with his arms to everyone he mentioned it to — until some grade twelve guys started making seagull squawking sounds whenever he walked by.

But Johnny is pretty handy to have around. When his parents' car broke down once as we were heading to the Woodstock Drive-In, Johnny popped the hood, did who knows what, and then we were on our way again. At least Jill will never have to worry about an unreliable vehicle.

In the fall, Johnny will start working full-time as a mechanic at his father's garage. His dad's current second-in-command, this old guy Eldon, has worked there for forty years and is ready to be done. So Johnny's set. He doesn't have to figure out a plan for himself and I don't think he'd want anything different, even if he could choose. His father is going to split everything with him, half-and-half. Jill is thrilled at the idea of Johnny being so quickly established and ready to support her (and then soon enough children). She's hoping more than anything for a diamond ring at Christmas.

Jill turns to me and smiles as the wedding party and all their family and friends approach. She takes my hand and squeezes it. I wink at her. I am her best friend. I know this is all she wants. She is mentally inserting herself in the scene. Jill is so sure she can make everything turn out the way she wants. I imagine she sees her life as a path lined with flowers — her favourite honeysuckle and phlox, cosmos and lupines all in bloom. She is sure the sun will shine more than it will rain. The flowers will grow strong and tall and lush, season after season. No one else will pick them. No deer will come and eat them or trample them down. Those flowers will surround her with beautiful colour and sweet fragrance as she skips along joyfully into the future.

It's getting late, going on midnight, when Jill finally puts away the pillowcases she's been embroidering for her hope chest and goes to bed. I sit on the cottage porch until I'm sure she's asleep. Then I get in the truck and drive up to the barn. The highway seems completely different without all the traffic. It is so quiet and peaceful. I turn in the store lot and park facing the road, close, only ten feet back from the shoulder. I turn the ignition off. Headlights off. Roll the window down. There are distant fireflies blinking, signalling to each other under the cover of the rose bushes at the base of the big sign. I imagine that Pepper Shaker inside heard the truck tires on the crushed rock, opened one eye, then went back to sleep. It's still. The stars are thumbtacked on the black bulletin board of the sky. The half moon glows above me, above the parking lot, the highway, the campsite, the river, Riverbend.

I wait. For something. Or nothing. I either want to see nothing or I want to see something unquestionable — unquestionably real. That deer I saw last night: its antlers weren't right for this time of year. Bucks lose their antlers in the late winter and then grow them new again. In the early summer, their antlers are going through the stages of regrowth, and they're smaller, velvety and soft, rounded, brown and knobby at the ends. That deer last night had sprawling sharp bony white antlers. I think. Maybe it was just the moonlight.

Or maybe it really was Speckles and maybe his antlers grow faster and whiter — another genetic abnormality. If he came down here again I could beep the truck horn to put a real scare in him, remind him the highway is dangerous. Send him running back to the forest.

Three transport trucks pass but otherwise nothing. I lean across to the passenger side and unroll the window. Earlier, Jill and I talked for almost two hours. She wanted to go over the wedding reception detail by detail. She tried to remember all the toasts that were made. The one that stuck out in my mind was the toast made by the bride's uncle: "To the start of your lives." Not to the start of your lives *together*. Just to the start of everything, as if by getting married these two people were pressing a reset button and nothing that happened to either of them before today counted.

The same general idea seems to come up in conversation with every adult you know the closer you get to finishing high school. They all want to know what you're doing after graduation to *start your life*. Like my life will really only get going after I head off to university. As if life up to now is only a practice run, or a warm-up for the main event. As if once I hit that glorious starting point sometime in the future, up to now erases. So when Bliss left, did he think he was starting his life? Restarting it? Did we, his family, and what he had experienced up to that point gradually dissipate or suddenly vanish — poof?

I'd like to ask him. I'd like to sit with him on the picnic table in front of the barn and have a big discussion about it. I wonder what happened at the start of his new story, where he went and why he went alone. Why, Bliss? Of course my parents are looking for answers, and I have to be patient. Although if I really stop to think it all through, it's like as they move forward with their search, my mind has been more and more determined to move back — to dig through my memories. As if I'm the one who's scared of forgetting things about him and his life before he left. Now that I'm here alone, it seems I'm sure I'll figure something out by travelling in reverse.

Something stirs outside.

A change in the air. Subtle, but I feel it.

I reach across the seat to grab the flashlight, and at the same time I hear the slight sound of air, wind, almost whistling, splitting apart to make way for something. I feel a breeze as if whatever it is has rushed by the window. Cold air. Cold-breath ghost? I jump out of the truck, circle it and begin to scan the parking lot. I hurry down the full length of it and back again. I shine the flashlight beam along the ground, looking for hoof prints. Side to side, side to side. Then I pass the beam of light along the wall of the barn.

Not far from the door there is a pair of glowing eyes. They are high off the ground, shining circles, reflecting the light.

I breathe in, stay as still as I can.

But the eyes are smaller than a deer would have and are closer together.

It is Pepper Shaker. Sitting in the barn window, looking out.

He, like me, probably wonders what on Earth I'm doing out here.

7

Three summers ago, Bliss tried to take off — to leave, at least for a little while. It happened one day after we'd been sitting together on the picnic table by the parking lot, watching customers. Bliss and I gave them names, identities and sometimes built up background stories for them. When we were younger there were a lot of spies, undercover detectives and private investigators who seemed to collect antiques. As we got older, we were more apt to figure that men were doctors or teachers and women were librarians or nurses. Bliss liked to guess that men were named Hubert or Humbert. If a woman was especially pretty I decided her name was likely Grace or Rose.

Then one morning I told Bliss I wouldn't rest until I saw the perfect Matilda. I have no idea why this idea popped into my head other than maybe from the heat of the day and mid-week boredom. I told Bliss that a Matilda probably had red or auburn hair, long, and not tied up. She'd be about our mother's age. She'd have glasses, which she would wear around her neck on a black cord, and cut-off jean shorts. I may as well have declared I was going to count pink cars. But later in the afternoon, as we sat sipping our pops, there she was. A brown station wagon hauling a little motorboat on a trailer parked near us. She got out. Her glasses were on her face, but she took them off as she stepped from the car, and sure enough, they were attached to a black necklace.

She flipped her long red hair out from under it. Her faded jean shorts had a purple flower-shaped patch on a back pocket.

Bliss wasn't paying attention. He was daydreaming, staring off to the highway. I elbowed him. Then I punched his arm.

"Hey, Vi, what?" he asked.

"Shhhhh. Matilda alert. Look," I whispered, and I tilted my head slightly in her direction.

"Freaky," Bliss said. He stared at her for several seconds. "Hey, Matilda," he called. I was mortified, and I was so sure she was going to turn around that I jumped off the picnic table, ready to dart before Bliss could embarrass me.

But she didn't acknowledge the name, and the man with her said, "Joan, hon, why don't you roll your window down? Let's leave them both open."

Joan? Bliss rolled his eyes.

I was already annoyed that he had called her name in the first place, so in retaliation I said loudly, "Hey Hubert, wait a sec."

The man turned to us. "Do I know you?" He looked sincerely puzzled.

No way. What were the chances?

A nervous giggle slipped out of me. After a few seconds too long I replied, "Oh, I was talking to my brother here."

Bliss could have helped me out but didn't. He stared off into the distance again as if he was suddenly focused on a tiny bird in a tree way across the highway. Hubert seemed to scrunch his eyebrows slightly, but then he and Joan went into the store.

As soon as Joan and Hubert were out of sight, Bliss got up and said he'd be right back. I figured he was going to the washroom. I stayed and when he didn't return after several minutes, I started to neaten the display of things outside the barn. I straightened an old hay rake that had fallen over. I turned several crocks around so their price tags were facing front. I refolded two antique quilts and carefully draped them over the rungs of an old wooden step ladder. The store was busy and customers went in and out as I tidied. Then an elderly couple stopped to talk to me about a glass washboard, and I knew it was too late to escape their nostalgic stranglehold once they started with, "When I was young." I nodded and smiled and eventually I caught a glimpse of Bliss coming back out of the barn.

When the couple went inside, I headed back to the picnic table. Bliss wasn't there. I scanned the parking lot and play area, but I didn't see him. Joan and Hubert's station wagon and boat were still parked in front of me, so they were obviously having a good look inside. I decided to stay and wait. Bliss would turn up.

I rolled up my shorts to get more sun on my legs. My tan was getting quite nice. The sun was naturally lightening up my brown hair too, unlike the peroxide disasters some girls inflicted on themselves. (There was one girl we all secretly called Penny, due to her horrid, copper hair. She was an annoying sort who claimed that whenever she gained any weight it went straight to her boobs. But I think it was just a ploy to get guys to buy her chocolate bars from the school canteen.) I thought about how I would actually love to have deep, rich, real auburn hair, when, as if I had subconsciously summoned her, beautiful, red-haired Joan came out of The Purple Barn. Hubert wasn't far behind. They stopped to look at the quilts I had folded and opened one up, holding it between them.

Where was Bliss? I didn't want to be sitting on the picnic table by myself when they got back in their car. I stood on the seat of the picnic table to get a better view of the parking lot. I could see over the top of Hubert and Joan's boat, well across the line of cars and campers, clear to the sign with the rose bushes and marigolds on the other side.

But no Bliss.

Then I heard something like a whistle, a single blast, maybe a bird call or tweet. I glanced to the playground, to the kids running around, one chasing a little dog, another pair throwing a Frisbee back and forth, to Joan and Hubert who were still holding the quilt, then to the highway. I heard the sound again. This time I knew for sure that it was a person whistling. It seemed to come from Joan and Hubert's boat. I was high enough up, standing on the seat of the picnic table, that just by leaning ahead a little bit I could look down into it.

There was Bliss, stretched out on the boat's floor. I would not have been much more surprised if I saw a mermaid lying there.

I whipped my head around to check on Joan and Hubert. They were starting to fold the quilt.

"Get out of there! Are you crazy?" I hissed to Bliss in my most forceful whisper. "They're going to be here any second."

He shrugged.

"It's not funny, come on!" Again I looked to Joan and Hubert. "What're you doing? Get out! Joke's over, Bliss." I was leaning so far ahead I had to jump off the picnic table seat.

"I'll be back," he said. "Don't worry, Vi."

I didn't know what to do. Joan and Hubert were approaching. Bliss wasn't budging. I was right at the side of the boat.

"They're coming. Get out!" I was too loud.

I heard a quizzical, "Hey," from Hubert behind me. He grimaced, and Joan, seemingly oblivious, put her glasses back on.

I quickly glanced back to the playground, to the kids playing Frisbee. Then I grabbed the side of the boat and took a deep breath.

"So did you get it?" I said loudly to Bliss, leaning ahead.

Without even daring to focus on their faces, I turned back to the approaching couple.

"Sorry," I said, "but our ball landed in your boat. My brother's getting it."

They stopped walking and stood just a few feet in front of me. I stared at Hubert's belt buckle. It was an odd thing, bright silver in the shape of a coiled snake.

"He's in there now?" Joan asked. She stretched her neck a little in my direction.

"Bliss, did you get it?" I asked again.

"I thought you said his name was Hubert," Hubert said.

I pretended not to hear him and turned to the boat. Bliss was standing now, lifting his leg over the opposite side to get out.

"Thanks," I said to Hubert and Joan. Then I turned and headed quickly into the store. Bliss followed me.

We walked through the store and went out the back door into the field. As we peeked around the corner of the barn, Hubert was backing out. The boat trailer was going crooked, and another car that was waiting for the parking spot had to move to give him more room.

I turned to Bliss.

"You wrecked my chance, Vi," he said.

"Not funny."

"You're right. I'm not laughing." The tone of his voice was different; he was annoyed. He'd been moody, distant, seemingly bored all week. I knew there was more to his response than me having spoiled his fun.

"So you were really going to take off with them?"

"I would've been back. I just wanted to try it, get away for a while — a little joyride. See how I'd feel. You know they would've stopped at Kings Landing, same as everyone, and I could've hitchhiked back." He wiped the sweat from his forehead then ran his hand through his hair.

I glanced up at a crow that cawed at us as it flew over.

"I'm going in," Bliss said. He began to walk away.

"Hey," I called. "You can't be mad, Bliss. You whistled, remember? If you wanted to go so bad and didn't want me saying anything, why'd you bother?"

He stopped but didn't turn around.

"Maybe I thought you'd come with me," he said.

"Really?" I shook my head, even though he couldn't see me.

He shrugged and continued walking.

"It wasn't cool, Bliss. Don't you think Mom and Dad would've been worried if you'd gone through with it? Don't —"

"Joyride, Vi," he said. He was almost to the back door of the barn. "That's it. End of story." Then he repeated himself, slowly and loudly, "Joy. Ride."

I've gone back to that afternoon so many times. Played it through in my mind to try to figure it out, if there really is some meaning to be found. Was it innocent fun? Or a practice run? What would I have thought if it had been anyone but Bliss? Did I overreact? Underreact?

As far as Bliss had gone that day, the idea of stowing away with a customer wasn't new. We had talked before about how easy it would be to slip into someone's camper and hang out and party in there all the way to the PEI ferry. Jokingly, of course. And Bliss always seemed to have a hundred imagined escapes for every one that I came up with.

The episode with the boat felt different somehow. It might have had something to do with Hubert. Like the coincidence of him meant something to Bliss, as if it was a cue to take action. There's graffiti that someone spray-painted on a flat surface of rock along the side of the highway not far from the barn that says "Take This as a Sign." Bliss always turned to look at it as we drove by, like a ritual, or a superstition. Even if we were in the middle of a conversation he would keep talking and turn to look. It had been there since we were little kids. Bright yellow lettering on the deep dark shale rock. Maybe Bliss had been waiting for a sign of his own and Hubert was it.

I should have listened more carefully to exactly what Bliss said. He said he wanted to go to see "how I'd feel." Not how it would feel, which I think is what most people would say. Most would wonder about the actual sensation of zooming down the highway in an open boat, wind blowing their hair, and the sun shining down. Bliss was wondering about how it would make him feel — and not just temporary exhilaration. For him it would have been a test, an experiment. He even clarified it for me. Joyride. Joy. Ride. Back then it was easy to assume his emphasis was on wanting the action, the ride, but now I'm sure he really wanted the emotion, the joy.

And did he really want me to go with him? To this day, I don't know. Maybe. That's what he said himself: maybe.

I do know that sometimes after you turn down one invitation, you don't get asked again.

8

Quinny's in the craft and souvenir section near the front of the store when I open the door of The Purple Barn. She's neatening our display of pet rocks and talking to a woman from Riverbend. Of course all the locals know Mrs. Quinn — the ones who come in to browse, to say hi or to use the barn as their entry point for a trip down memory lane. Quinny chats them up and always has bits of gossip to share. She's nosy and seems to know as much as the receptionist at the doctor's office, the high school secretary and all three bank tellers put together.

I'm tired and my plan is to walk directly to the stool behind the counter, sit and listen to the radio. I hope I can perk myself up a bit after my five-hour sleep, which seems to be my average lately. But Quinny notices me before I can slip past her.

"Your father —" she starts.

"He called?"

"No, but when he calls next, I'd like to speak to him as well, about the estate. So if you happen to pick up —"

"Sure," I say. I want to start walking again, but Quinny has taken a step and is blocking my way.

"Do you think we'll hear from him soon? I certainly understand that they're vacationing and it's well-deserved time away, but they did choose our busiest time of year to travel and the business —"

"I'm sure he'll check in soon. He said he would."

Quinny hesitates at first, then goes. She sure seems determined to see the estate. The way she's acting you wouldn't think it was a cottage full of old household things but a fabric store liquidation.

Around eleven I let Pepper Shaker chase around an antique tin wind-up monkey for a while, then I head outside. I get a Cream Soda from the pop machine for Dean and me to share. (It's a flavour I don't have in my stash in the stream.) Dean's raking the parking lot and pulling the few weeds he finds. It looks like there's something sprouting from his pocket with the green dandelion leaves sticking out. Dean keeps the whole outside of the barn looking pretty much as perfect as the day we had the photo taken for our tourist brochure. He does everything he can think of to keep the property at its best without being asked. I know it's out of loyalty to Bliss, and to my parents and me, but he's also a good, nice guy. It sounds so simple to say, but it's true. He's the kind of guy that grandmothers like.

Dean's already finished his first year of an engineering degree from the university in Fredericton. He could have stayed in the city for the summer and found a job there. He probably could have even found something related to his studies, something that would look good to future employers. I know my father's paying him well to work at the barn, but Dean says he wanted to be home for the summer to be with me.

I call to him and he drags the rake back and forth a couple more times, then leans it against the side of the barn. As he walks towards me, I notice a woman getting out of a car glance sideways to check him out.

"Cream Soda, eh? You know I've always thought that stuff tastes like liquid bubble gum." He takes a long drink before handing the bottle back to me. "Listen," he says. "Go ahead back to the woods and I'll be right there. Don't get too excited, but I brought you something."

I walk across the meadow to the edge of the forest. The shade of the branches feels nice as I step into the line of trees. I sit at the edge of the stream. I kick off my sandals and put my toes in the water.

Dean is carrying a brown paper grocery bag folded in half. It seems so flat that I'd think it was empty if he hadn't already told me there was something for me inside it.

He sits down close beside me and rests his feet on a rock at the stream's edge.

"Now it's not exactly —" he begins, but I open the bag so quickly he stops.

Inside is a 1907 calendar with a watercolour print of a cardinal perched on a crabapple branch.

"Look where it's from," Dean says. He points and reads, "Haventon Dry Goods." Haventon is the name of the drowned town. "I got it from my old uncle Les," he says.

"That's the uncle you went to visit the other night? I thought you didn't like going there because all he ever wants to do is play cards while he goes on and on about his heart condition."

"It took four games of crib to get that for you. I remembered seeing it once in his shed. He worked there as a kid."

"And you got it for the store's booth at Community Days?"

He nods.

"It's perfect. Thanks."

"So," he says. "Any chance you'll trade me all those old dates for one new date?" He glances down at the calendar then looks up at me and smiles.

"You've been working on that line all day, haven't you?"

"Maybe. But what do you think? We haven't gone out anywhere good for a while. And you're supposed to be having fun this summer, right? I can't leave that completely up to Jill."

"How about Friday night then? We'll think up something cool to do and after," — I wink and hold up my right hand with my index finger pointed for emphasis — "as long as you preserve my good name and remind your mom that the cottage has not only two bedrooms but a couch, you can even come for a little overnight visit."

He smiles. "An offer I can't refuse," he says. Then he leans in close and gives me a kiss. His tiny moustache tickles like a mosquito dancing along my skin and I laugh.

"That thrilling, eh?" he says.

"Sorry. Try me again. I'll brace myself."

This time he puts a hand gently on my cheek and runs the other through my hair. He kisses me softly, then he leans in so close my chest is against him. He kisses me longer until he stops suddenly and pulls back, tilts his head.

"Hey," I say. "What?"

He listens for a few seconds then shakes his head. "Nothing, I guess. I just thought —"

I lean in to him and put my lips on his, and then I hear a rustle in the tall grass in the meadow. A dark shadow appears in my periphery.

It's Quinny.

The sun behind her is making her grey pouffed hair glow and shine as if it's a tinfoil ball full of Jiffy Pop. Her face is flushed. She's probably embarrassed. For me, that is.

"Dean," she says, with perfect authority, without the slightest waver in her voice. "A customer has purchased an entire bedroom set and most certainly cannot load it without your assistance. You go right now as they've already been waiting while I've tried to track you down." I can tell by the way she's holding her lips just so, that she'd like to add another line or two, perhaps tag a moral on to the end of this story, but he doesn't give her a chance. He stands up and takes off to the barn.

Quinny looks at me next. She pushes her glasses up the bridge of her nose. A piece of her hair has slipped loose and twists outward like a tentacle. Quinny's told me before that her first kiss was at the altar. But I guess that's how it went in the 1930s. I swear being around all these antiques has made her think time has stopped. She's the perfect candidate for getting tangled in a time warp.

"Was it the oak one or the stencilled pine?" I ask.

She's looking at my halter top strap, which has slipped off my shoulder. I fix it.

"The bedroom set. Was it —"

"The pine," she says. "And they paid full price, no quibble. I must get back."

She turns and hurries across the meadow to the barn.

Alone again. I slip my sandals on and sit up in the lawn chair. I figure I'll take a little breather before I rush back to Quinny's side in the store. Let some of the smell of sin waft off me first. I watch the water trickle in the stream and try to think of absolutely nothing. Then a twig snaps in the distance — a teeny tiny snap surely caused by nothing bigger than a chipmunk — but my mind jumps to the conclusion it could have been a deer. A deer like Speckles. Speckles the moonlight wanderer. Speckles the white of the night.

Even though we only saw Speckles a dozen or so times over the years, Bliss mentioned him often. Since what we first read in the encyclopedia about piebald deer didn't make it clear, Bliss used to wonder if Speckles was born looking the way he does or if he changed as he grew. Like all fawns' spots disappear. Like my hair was white blond when I was little and now it's brown. Sometimes things change for the better as we grow up, and sometimes things change for the worse. Like Lorna Lee Roberts, this girl at school whose spine gradually twisted as she grew taller. Like Jill's cousin who had the prettiest pearly baby teeth, but then her permanent ones came in yellowish and crooked.

Flaws can come out. Just the same as puberty hits when your body decides it's time, other unpleasant surprises can be lurking inside you waiting for their chance to strike, for their genes to switch on. Something that was always there, a condition or an illness you were born with, shows itself. And no matter how badly you might want to, these things can't be controlled or changed. I realize that now.

I take the calendar Dean gave me and head to the barn. I want to avoid an awkward conversation with Quinny, so I go in the back door and right into The Room. I set the calendar on the shelf with the few other things I've gathered so far for The Purple Barn's booth in the arena during Riverbend Community Days. I make a special display every year. I suppose it's my way to be a collector. Mom used to help when I was younger, but for the past four years I've been completely in charge. I try to think of an interesting theme that even people who figure they don't like antiques might want to look at. One year I gathered dozens of old brass bells, all different, from cowbells to railway bells to a large schoolhouse bell. And of course people loved to pick them up and ring them. One year I had a display of fountain pens people could try. Once it was antique ladies' hats. I had a big mirror and there were lots of laughs as people modelled them.

This year is the tenth anniversary that The Purple Barn's been in business, and it's been ten years since the dam and permanent flood. I'm gathering old things from the drowned town of Haventon — items printed with the actual town name since you don't see it anywhere anymore. It hasn't been as easy finding stuff as I thought it would be. Including the calendar, I have a grand total of five things. I'd love to get more, and at least one show-stopping something, though I have no idea what it would be. At least I still have plenty of time before the Labour Day weekend when Community Days start. Deciding what to search for is one thing, finding what you want is another altogether.

. . .

I head back to the barn's sales floor just as Elizabeth comes with my lunch. She's balancing a tinfoil-covered plate on top of a tin (which I'm going to guess has a treat for Dean inside) and has her purse and another bag besides. I help her carry everything to the storage room.

Once we're inside she says in a low voice, "So Mrs. Quinn told you about the estate, right? Do you think it will be strange to go?"

"Without Dad? No, I'm good."

Elizabeth nods slightly. "Mrs. Quinn didn't tell you where it is, did she Vi?"

I shake my head and realize that "where" must mean far more than simply the address.

"If your father could only choose one more estate to buy around here — ever — what one would it be?" Elizabeth asks.

"The Vaughn place?"

Elizabeth smiles.

Not a cottage, but *the cottage*. That explains everything.

The Vaughn cottage on Pine Lake has been boarded up and abandoned for fifteen years. What used to be a pretty beach with trucked-in sand along the waterfront has been mostly washed away or taken over by grass, weeds and alder bushes. The forested section of the considerable acreage that would be the equivalent of ten camp lots today is creeping ever closer to the building. Like most people who've been on the lake, I've seen the big "No Trespassing" and "Private Property" signs. Johnny's dad has a boat, and he took Jill and me out one day a couple of summers ago. We floated along close to the shore to see what we could of the place, but it wasn't much. Branches blocked our view from every angle. And I'm sure it's even more grown over now.

The Vaughn place was the first one built on Pine Lake. Calling it a cottage is a bit of an understatement. It's a big storey-and-a-half house. The original Mr. Vaughn was a rich businessman from Ontario whose family owned a bottle manufacturing plant. He came down to our area for a summer holiday and met the future Mrs. Vaughn — Ivy Swan, an only child, a New Brunswick beauty. As an engagement gift, and enticement for her to leave home and move with him to Ontario, he bought the land at the lake and built the cottage.

No expense or detail was spared in furnishing it. Ivy bought everything she wanted and more. Crates and boxes came from Eaton's and from expensive furniture stores in Boston and New York. She had gorgeous china for everyday — Limoges dishes straight from France. She had cranberry and Vaseline glass lemonade sets and candy dishes, silverware, gold-trimmed cake and dessert stands and monogrammed linens.

When the cottage was complete and all set up just so, Ivy had a ladies' tea. It was an afternoon affair that every woman in the area was invited to, and then talked about for years. Ivy was said to be gracious and wonderful, elegantly dressed and the perfect hostess. Plus the glorious things inside the cottage that had been previously only rumoured to exist, were seen first-hand. Ivy became local royalty.

The Vaughns returned every summer. Ivy was spotted year after year, friendly and chatting, at the grocery store, church or at the annual community picnic. She had children, then grandchildren. It seemed she never lost her love for the area or her desire to come back to her beautiful summer home — for more than fifty years.

But then one August there was an accident. A teenage boy, a Vaughn grandson, drowned on the far side of the lake. The family left to bury him at home in Ontario, and the cottage was boarded up within days. Cecil Haines, who was their winter caretaker, got the call to do it. He covered every window pane with a perfectly cut piece of plywood. No one knew if the family thought they'd come back, the next summer or someday, or if they planned to sell it. Locals watched for them the next year. Then the next. Nothing changed. People thought Ivy would come back again, and maybe she would have, but she died before returning. Cecil still checks the cottage to ensure that a January snowfall doesn't collapse the roof or a family of raccoons doesn't take up residence in one of the bedrooms. The inside is reportedly exactly the same as when the family left.

Time stopped at the cottage fifteen summers ago. And as years went by, the tragedy of the place faded in everyone's memory — as seems to happen often with sadness that is not our own. But the local interest in Ivy's story didn't dissipate. People had wondered about the legendary cottage and everything inside it for generations. The boarded-up windows just made it seem even more like a locked treasure chest. Curiosity doesn't fade — it sometimes grows stronger.

"So of course Quinny wants to go with you," Jill says. We're sitting on opposite ends of the couch in our cabin, sharing a bowl of popcorn. Jill's working on an embroidered pillowcase. She is stitching dainty blue forget-me-nots around the pink word "Hers."

"Seeing inside that place would not only lock her in as Riverbend's Queen of Gossip, but probably extend her reign to all of York County," I say.

"Oh, I can just see it," Jill says and starts to giggle. "You two driving there together. Quinny in the truck riding shotgun."

I throw a piece of popcorn at her. "Yeah. Highly unlikely."

"You don't think she'll be able to convince your dad? Quinny versus Foster? Foster the Hermit? I don't know."

"Not worried. I mean, picture this, who'd make a better bodyguard for little me: Quinny or Foster?"

"I suppose," Jill says. "But I bet Quinny could easily conceal a weapon in that hairdo of hers."

I get a quick visual of Quinny raising her hand to her head and pulling out a long shiny carving knife.

After we quit giggling, Jill admits she does understand it though — the interest, the nosiness. It really is human nature. At Kings Landing she can sometimes see the delight people take in being able to wander through houses room by room. And sometimes curiosity is just that, and a look is enough, but so often that interest leads to desire.

"Poor, poor Quinny," Jill says. "Mean ol' Violet is banning her completely, taking all her fun away." She shakes her head with a pouty look on her face and pretends to wipe away a tear. But then she asks if I remember that old nut job Mr. Vernon and the deal with his estate. That was a different story entirely.

Mr. Vernon died three years ago. He was eighty-five and living alone. His wife had died at least twenty years before, and they never had any children. He lived in Dumfries in a big two-storey house. Mr. Vernon wasn't around much, but sometimes he'd be in the Save-Easy buying groceries, or we'd see his unmistakable old blue-and-white boat of an Oldsmobile going down the highway, slow and low, as if he was the Honorary Grand Marshal of the Riverbend Canada Day parade, and the backed-up campers and transport trucks behind him were the floats. Sometimes he was in his yard as we went by his house. He'd be out trimming branches or mowing the lawn or weeding the flower bed that lined the long driveway.

Mr. Vernon was harmless, but sane or senile, there was one odd bit of information about him that everyone knew. As he got older, he became insistent that after he died his whole house be burned — contents and all. It was his stuff, his life, and he had no heirs, so he didn't need anyone in there nosing around his underwear drawer looking for tucked-away secrets once he was gone. If he was dead then he had no use for any of it anymore. And since he was the only one who ever needed the stuff during his life, then he didn't see how anyone else needed any of it after his death. The word around here was that he would have liked to torch it himself. But unless he collapsed from a heart attack or stroke with a lit match in his hand, it wasn't happening.

He made a deal with the fire department. Mr. Vernon paid them a lot of money, much more than was necessary apparently, and he and the chief shook on it. The firemen would use the burning as a training exercise. Of course there were rumours that Mr. Vernon wanted his house burned because he had something to hide. Quinny suggested that surely if the things were given to the church instead, to pass along to the less fortunate, some good could come of it. Some women remembered his wife's beautiful collection of china cups and saucers, no two the same, and oh what a sin, and oh, what would she think. But really, no one could stop him.

Mr. Vernon died. And was buried. Then out of nowhere, a great-niece of Mr. Vernon's pops up and calls Dad at the store. She tells him she has a discreet proposition for him. She has a key to the dead man's house. A thousand dollars will buy a turn of that key and a trip inside to take what he wants (nothing too obvious that the firemen may notice missing, but he could go ahead and fill boxes with china, silver, whatever). Pay your money, take your chances.

She turned a little nasty when Dad said no. She threatened that if he said a word to anyone, she'd say that actually he had approached her. My father phoned up one of the volunteer firefighters and gave him some cash to guard the place until it was burned. Dad told Mom he would have loved to see what was in the house and God knows what treasures would be torched, but it wasn't his decision to make.

. . .

As far as the Vaughn place goes, Dad has been curious about it forever. When we were younger and Mom asked us what we wanted to do on a Sunday afternoon, Dad would occasionally answer with a wink and say, "Go take a little tour of the Vaughn cottage." So now it's up to me to go on his behalf, seize his opportunity for him — for us. It's my chance to prove that I can keep things running here not only business-as-usual, but better than usual. And I won't lie, I wonder what's behind the walls and boarded-up windows too.

Really, so many of the objects I'm surrounded by every day, the items in the store, ended up here because of a death. It's true that you can't take it with you, and something has to be done with all the things we leave behind. Families keep what they want from an estate, but there is often more left over. Our stock is what remains.

At least the things in our store usually come from the estates of old people. But just because you're old doesn't mean your death isn't a tragedy. I don't think anyone plans on dying the day they die, so essentially everyone's life is cut short. Does anyone leave their house clean every time they go out in case they die of an aneurysm, the same way they never wear underwear with holes in case they're in an accident? Does anyone ask themselves: If you died today, would you be ready to have your house rummaged through? Where are your *Playboy* magazines? Your hair dye? Your Ex-Lax? That holey underwear? Your pills? Your wig? Your everything. Every *thing*. All your stuff, your secrets.

What would you want people to have? Do you think they could ever guess right? Everything we own has a reason for being with us. We bought it, it was a Christmas gift, we found it, we made it, we inherited it, someone left it at our place. But even we can forget where the things we have came from, and their meaning changes in time.

It's understandable that an heir would keep something like a special piece of jewellery that the former owner wore often, but I think sometimes people are a little too eager with their declarations of sentimental value. Things are things, nothing more, regardless of who owned them, touched them, kept them sitting on a shelf in the background of their life. A cup and saucer owned by your grandmother should be no more important than any other cup and saucer simply because she spent twenty-five cents to buy it on some insignificant trip to Fredericton, and she liked the roses on it better than the green ferns on the only other one in the store that was marked down, and she had just wanted a little something as a pick-me-up since the kids were driving her crazy. A vase of your dead aunt's that you love she may have hated, and perhaps she kept it only so the neighbour who gave it to her would see it in use. She may be rolling in her grave, thinking of you making it seem as if she had such terrible taste. It's okay if it's special to you, but it's wrong to assume it was special to her.

The emotional attachment that comes with sentimental value is for the person who owns an object now — not who owned it before. Sometimes I think sentimental value is for people who can't be confident enough in their memories. Having a reminder, a souvenir, to help you remember is great, but I think the best memories are through a special door in your mind that you can open without a key.

Or maybe it's that we keep some of a loved one's possessions after they've died as a way to deal with what we can't understand. We want to have an object they owned out where we can see it. We want to be sure we know where a few of their things are, because we don't truly know — can't fathom — where they themselves have gone.

Jill is in the kitchen getting more popcorn when there's a knock at the door. Our neighbour is standing on the porch.

"Sorry to bother you, but I was wondering if you could move your truck over," he says. "I can't get my car in."

I glance at our shared driveway between the two cabins. I did pull in a little wide. "Sure," I say.

"Thanks." He half nods, then he turns quickly without saying anything else. He gets in his car and waits.

When I'm back inside Jill is in the living room again.

"Have you talked to him at all?" I ask her.

"No. He did wave at me the other day, though. Before I didn't think he seemed friendly, but I think he's just shy and keeps to himself."

"I suppose. Not that it matters, but I wondered," I say.

"Dwayne thinks he might be taking a summer course at the university in Fredericton."

The mention of the university makes me think of Dean and our date and evening visit. So I tell Jill, and she says she'll stay over at her house in Riverbend on Friday night. Dean and I will be alone.

9

Quinny's on the phone with my father when I arrive at the store.

"Such a well-to-do family though, Mr. Davis," she says.

She doesn't turn to look at me, so I stop by our big New Brunswick map to listen.

"But my goodness, with all due respect."

There's a long pause and then finally she says, "Yes, of course, I understand." But her fingers are tapping rapidly on the counter with such force that I notice little waves forming in the vase of flowers.

I walk to where she can see me and I point at the phone and mouth, My father?

She nods, and after a bit more conversation it's my turn. Quinny walks out onto the display floor, leaving me alone to talk.

"You're shattering her ice-cold heart," I say to him. "Grounding her."

Dad laughs. I love the sound of it.

"Violet, I tell you, if I was away for any other reason I'd turn around and come straight back. Buy it all. Don't let them change their mind or offer it to anyone else. Pay whatever you need to. And once you have everything, get Foster to fit what you can in The Room, then put the rest in the garage at the house."

"I will. Don't worry. I'll get it."

"You know I miss you, right?" Dad says.

"You too. And Mom. Have you —"

"No." A pause. "No, we don't have any leads. Not yet." Another pause and I bet anything he's turned to look at Mom, give her a little smile, maybe squeeze her hand.

"Okay," I say. I try to keep the sound of disappointment out of my voice.

"So you're all doing good? Jill and Dean too?" Then he goes on, "Since you're doing this big job of the estate for me, why don't you pay yourself a little extra and take them out this weekend. This is Old Home Week up in Woodstock right? Go have fun — my treat. Oh, just a sec —"

I can hear Mom telling him something.

"Your mom thinks it's a great idea. Go on all the rides, she says. Have fun. It would mean a lot to us."

I tell him sure and I know he's so relieved — pleased even. I tell them I love them and say goodbye. At least they know that one of their children is accounted for. And trying to be happy.

Once I'm off the phone, Quinny tells me she's pleased that my parents are enjoying their vacation, and then in the same breath she says she'll work the cash and I should make myself useful elsewhere. I walk directly to The Room. Quinny watches me go. I wonder if she'll really be able to bite her tongue and not complain about my father thwarting her potential gossip coup of the decade. She's always been respectful of my father and is well aware that the fact he's chosen her to work here has given her a certain status in the community.

In The Room I move things around to make the most space I can for new acquisitions. It's a large room, about twelve feet wide and at least twenty-five long. I slide and shove and stack everything the best I can against the far wall. Then I lift boxes of inventory from the floor onto tables. I drag and push a heavy cedar chest. I stack a set of six wooden hoop-back chairs in two groups of three.

"Violet," Quinny says sternly through the door, "Mr. Kensey has delivered a load of his —" she pauses to think of the right word, and I realize that Foster must be there too. "Handiwork," she finishes. "And before he leaves I know you have details to give him about your outing on Saturday."

I open the door and see Foster standing by the brochure rack. His *handiwork*, his heart-trimmed twig art tables, are in front of the counter, and Dean is gradually moving the little tables into the display. Dean winks at me. Quinny doesn't notice because she's glaring at Foster and follows me towards him.

"Violet," he says.

"This Saturday, ten o'clock we'll head out. You meet me here? It's the old Vaughn place."

"You mean down at the lake? Can't say I was expecting that."

You know a place truly is legendary when someone as far out of the loop as Foster Kensey has heard of it.

"Good enough then." He turns to go, but Quinny pipes up.

"And Mr. Kensey," she says, "on behalf of Mr. Davis, if I may ask that you do your best to present yourself in a neat and well-kept manner."

Right. I love how Quinny even suggests that it's for my father's benefit. She is so crazy annoyed she's not going. And that Foster, of all people, is. I would never have been so rude to suggest it, but a bit of sprucing up on Foster's part wouldn't hurt anything. I know Dwayne has mentioned to Foster in the past that he can take a proper shower at Seven Birches if he ever wants to.

Foster simply nods at her, then me, and turns to leave. As he goes out the front door a customer comes in with one of his twig tables that she must have taken from the display outside. She seems a little startled by Foster and steps wide of him. I wonder if she'd believe that he's the artist of the piece she's about to acquire.

. . .

One of our regular customers, Mrs. Harris, comes in mid-afternoon. She's the grade ten typing teacher at school. She's the sort whose bathroom probably is the exact colour of the barn. You know, with little magenta ceramic fish plaques along the wall, and pink toilet paper and dozens of Avon bottles of perfumes and lotions lined up on the counter. She wears eyeshadow in a rainbow arc of layers and paints her nails. They're usually a bright pinkish-orange, and they dance like flames above the typewriter keys as she demonstrates the proper technique. She loves huge billowing dresses and is always wearing something floral patterned — never decorated with anything dainty like forget-me-nots, but giant red, orange or yellow tropical flowers. She's a distant cousin of Quinny's.

Mrs. Harris is in checking if we have any new spaghetti poodles. She collects them. They're little department store china trinkets with "fur" that resembles miniature pottery spaghetti noodles. The dogs are usually pink or white and trimmed with a bit of gold. They're only from the 1950s, not really that old at all, but once Dad found out she likes them, he never passes up a chance to buy one. She gets excited and coos — "Oh, my new wee doggie" — whenever he shows her a poodle he's found.

And of course she also stops in just to chat with Quinny. I don't need to hear much of their conversation to realize that Quinny has already turned the Vaughn estate situation around in her mind and made the latest information work in her favour. I overhear her saying that of course with my father being away, *she* is the one the estate owners have been in contact with and is handling the details. My job description has been reconfigured to sound as if I'm simply driving down to the place and handing over a cheque. When Mrs. Harris asks when the estate items will finally be for sale in the store, Quinny clarifies that it will only be after my parents return home from vacation—at which time she will graciously assist with the unpacking, sorting and pricing of items.

These are the details Quinny repeats again on Thursday. And Friday. Locals are gradually trickling in, all claiming they just wanted to stop by, hadn't been in for a while. Quinny's spreading the word, and no matter how she tells the story it will be good for business. Lots of people wonder what's behind the Vaughn estate's boarded-up windows. For some, just seeing a few items in the store will satisfy their curiosity. For others, they'll want to buy something, take it home, display it and use it as a conversation starter to impress guests. The story of where an item came from, its history, is called provenance in the antiques business. And around here, an item from the Vaughn cottage has the ultimate provenance.

I take Dad's suggestion of going to Old Home Week for my date with Dean. Jill and Johnny come too. Johnny drives, so Jill and I split a bottle of Baby Duck on the way there. We leave Riverbend at five thirty and Johnny takes the back road, so we make it to Woodstock a little after six.

The fair is packed. Even with the harness racing going on and hundreds of people sitting in the stands, all the rides, games, exhibition halls—and especially the Bingo tent—are busy. Johnny and Dean want to play some of the shooting games, so Jill and I look at the crafts and 4-H displays first. That will give the wine a while to soak into our systems, to make sure there's no embarrassing barfing on the Zipper or Tilt-a-Whirl.

We walk by long tables filled with endless varieties of jam, jelly, relish and pickles. Almost every jar seems to have been awarded a colourful ribbon—first, second, third or many honourable mentions.

The next tables display cookies, squares and pies, then floral bouquets, then mittens and socks (mostly made of variegated yarn), crocheted granny square pillows and afghans, embroidered pillowcases and framed cross-stitches. Jill stops to admire some tea towels decorated with little blue birds: one holds a teapot in its beak and another holds a cup. I can tell she's added to her hope chest project list by the way she says, "Aw, Vi, look. Sooo cute." We see homemade Barbie doll clothes, a pair of sock monkeys and finally a display of quilts draped over a long clothesline running high all along the end wall. Ribbons hang on almost every quilt as well, the skinny strips of red, blue, white or yellow. But there is one ribbon that looks like it would be about five yards long if unravelled. It is pink and is twisted and tucked and bowed into a flower shape with six strands hanging down from it. Jill elbows me when she sees it. It says "Best in Show," and of course the quilt it's hanging from has a card that reads "Alvina Quinn."

We're looking at the incubator of freshly hatched chicks in the 4-H section when Dean and Johnny meet up with us. Even though there's a sign that says "Don't Touch the Chicks," kids are patting, cuddling, tapping and almost squishing the little yellow puffballs. We go outside and ride the Paratrooper first, then the Spider, the Scrambler, the Tilt-a-Whirl and finally the Zipper (twice). I love the speed, the spinning, the twist and the whoosh, the unusual feeling of being upside-down, sideways, here and then there all in a matter of seconds. We do the bumper cars. We bet on the birthday wheel and Jill wins ten dollars. We try the water gun car race, buy a corn dog, candy apple and finally a vanilla and chocolate twist cone. We wander back to the parking lot and sit on the hood of the car to eat our ice cream.

"You know it would've been great to have Bliss here tonight," Johnny says. "It sometimes took a lot of convincing to get him going, but he was always cool to have along."

"Yeah, for sure," Dean says. He puts his arm around me.

"You remember that time the three of us got stuck at the top of the Ferris wheel?" Johnny asks.

"And we all took turns climbing on the roof of our car? Bliss swore we could see the Maine border from up there," Dean says.

"Oh yeah." Johnny nods again and again. "Good times."

Dean leans in and kisses my cheek.

"Well if you don't mind, Johnny boy," he says, "I think it's about time we head on out."

I think of what Johnny said about Bliss on the way home. He did try to be happy, even when he was actually feeling far from it. The awful gloom that came over him that Christmas Day did return — again and again. It hovered and circled and then without warning could suddenly blow like a gust of wind into his ear, sending any notion or memory he had of how to be happy swirling away, loosening old bad thoughts, lifting feelings of sorrow and guilt up to the forefront of his mind.

One Saturday in November when Bliss was thirteen and I was twelve, we went with Mom for groceries at the Riverbend Save-Easy. A big Pontiac was parked in the lot with a giant buck splayed across the hood. Several men were standing around it, talking and smoking. One man was wearing a hunting cap, so he was obviously the host of the show and tell. His name was Ed Price, a guy Jill's dad knew. He was leaning against the passenger side door.

We walked by the car and the buck to go inside the store. I glanced quickly past it. Bliss did too.

But Mr. Price called to him, "Hey young fella, you ever seen one this size? I've been hunting since I was probably your age, and it's the biggest I ever got."

Bliss turned. "Cool," he said.

Mom was her usual gracious self and stopped. "It's certainly the largest I've seen. Looks like nice steaks and stews all winter for you." I'm pretty sure that, like us, she'd never had a bite of venison in her life.

Bliss kept walking. So did I.

"Well, it seems as if these two are in a hurry," Mom said. I looked back and saw her smile and shake her head. Then she followed us in.

When we were back in the car after shopping, Mom spoke to Bliss. I sat in the front passenger seat and he was in the back.

"I know you've been a Grumpy Gus lately, but that is certainly no reason to forget your manners. It would have taken you all of three seconds to step closer to that buck and say congratulations," Mom said. She looked into the rear-view mirror back at Bliss. Public perception counted a lot with Mom. "You have to think of the feelings of other people. And maybe you'd be able to cheer up a little if you shared in someone else's happiness."

Bliss didn't say anything. I turned around and he was looking out the window.

"Mom, the deer was dead," I said. "That's not really anything to be happy about."

"Enough, Violet," she said. "You know what I mean. It's about making an effort."

She looked in the rear-view mirror again.

Bliss still remained silent.

Mom began to drive. No one spoke until we pulled into our driveway and parked.

Mom took the keys out of the ignition. "Don't get out just yet," she said.

She set the keys on her lap and focused on them. "Bliss, you know

I love you." She paused. "You know you can talk to someone if you think it would help you feel better."

I glanced at her. She didn't look up. She was pushing a key back and forth with her index finger.

"I know you said before you didn't want to talk to Minister Blake," Mom went on. "But, I don't know, I mean, I'm not sure I understand it all exactly, but, you could try maybe —" she looked up and I thought she was going to turn to Bliss, but instead she stared out the window. "What if you talked to a doctor?"

"What, and get a cast on my head or something?" Bliss said. "Yeah, I'm sure that would help."

I turned around and Bliss sniffed, tilted his head way back against the seat and looked up to the car's ceiling. I knew that as soon as he'd snapped at Mom he felt bad.

"Don't worry, okay," he said without shifting his gaze. "It'll be fine. Go ahead and open the trunk and I'll bring all the groceries in."

When we finished putting everything away, I went to talk to Bliss in his room. He was lying on his bed. I sat on the end of it and leaned against the footboard.

"You okay?"

He nodded.

"You know Mom just wants to help."

"I know."

"What are you thinking about?"

He shrugged. "Stuff."

I knew that meant the boneyard — the unforgettable flaw of the forest. The memory of it didn't fade as he got older, like it should have, and likely would have in someone else. I think every time he remembered it, the impact grew stronger.

. . .

I had gradually realized that you could indeed have an emotion without a cause — or at least Bliss could. The boneyard wasn't what made him feel bad in the first place, but the memory of it was always right there, ready to pounce once he did. When his mind twisted and he felt sad for seemingly no immediate reason, the memory of the boneyard was always available, offering itself as a logical (although truly illogical) conclusion. It became a horrible cycle. Struggling with his impaired brain trying to make sense of senseless emotions only resulted in him despairing more.

From what he'd said over the years, I knew that as a child Bliss felt helpless when it came to the boneyard. He hadn't believed it existed, felt awful when he found out it did — and discovered so many beautiful deer tossed like trash — but he could do nothing to change any of it. He (wrongly) felt guilty thinking he had left something undone, figured he should have (impossibly) acted somehow. The boneyard was his first proof of unhappy endings.

And of course it wasn't only the boneyard that came back to him when the feelings of gloom took over. His turmoil was far from that simple or singular. It seemed that every bad memory, in fact only bad memories, bubbled up in his brain. His entire perspective changed and every thought he had was permeated and tainted, shifted and reinterpreted in a negative way. But he'd carried his distorted recollection of the boneyard as something he should feel badly about the longest, so it always loomed large and was the strongest.

"You know there's nothing back there to feel bad about," I said — the same as always. "You don't have to try to make sense of anything. Maybe if you stop thinking about why you might feel bad, you'll be able to stop the feeling too."

"It'd be nice," he said. "It's not like I want to dwell on this."

"So why don't you? You're strong, Bliss. Believe me, I have been with you your whole life and there is nothing in your past worth upsetting yourself about. You're a good, good person. I wouldn't lie to you. You should tell yourself your mind is making a mistake and lying. Because it is — you know that. I know that. Tell yourself to stop it."

He ran his hand through his hair. Then he pushed himself up into a sitting position and leaned against the headboard.

"Slide over closer for a minute, Vi, sit right here in front of me," he said. "And I don't want you to move — at all. And you're not allowed to close your eyes. Just look right at me."

"Okay," I said.

"Now, I want you to stop seeing me," Bliss said.

"What? You just said I can't close my eyes or move. What, are you going to disappear or something?"

"No," he said. "No, not at all. It's up to you. Control it yourself. Just tell your mind to stop seeing me. You're strong, Vi. Think real hard and stop it."

I got goosebumps.

"It's impossible," I said.

"It is. But I swear I try though, Vi, I do. I really do."

I did close my eyes then and took a deep breath to refocus myself.

"But it's me that has to do this — work it out," Bliss said. "Talking to someone else isn't going to help."

I looked down and traced a line of stitching in the bedspread with my finger. He had to be exaggerating, right? He had to be. He obviously just hadn't figured out the right way to control it yet. He wasn't crazy. Surely he'd get better as he got older, stronger, smarter.

I looked back up at him. "But it does go away on its own, at least after a while?" I asked. "You feel better and back to normal eventually?"

"So far, yes," he said, nodding slowly.

So far — yes.

Johnny and Jill drop Dean and me off at the campsite. I grab us each a beer from the fridge and we sit in the rocking chairs on the porch. The sun is almost completely gone now, glowing a pinkish red, low across the river, the slight bump of it showing above the distant trees, just beyond Riverbend. Rosy-tinged clouds, a line of colour, hover like a long, unwound piece of cotton candy. I hear the distant chatter of people at their campsites, and the hum of vehicles rolling along the highway. A few people are still jumping, splashing and laughing in the pool. The lights around the pool are on, and the Christmas lights are plugged in on the trees near the washrooms. The red and green does look a little odd, but Dwayne wanted them left up to add a bit of festive fun to the place, even though Christmas in July is officially over.

Dean and I replay the highs and lows of the fair, rocking in the rockers. We drink more beer. The sun disappears completely and the traffic on the highway thins out. The periods of silence between the sounds of cars and big transports rolling by gradually increase. The pool closes. Campfires are put out. It is dark except for the lights on the washroom building and the decorated trees.

We go inside. The cottage is cool. I close the tiny window above the kitchen sink and head to the one on the side of the living room. Dean sits on the couch. I pull back the curtains to slide the window closed. We've left the lights off inside so it's easy to see out. A man is walking, leaving the washroom building. He's got a backpack and long pants and even a coat and cap. It's Foster. He came down to take a real shower. I wonder if it was his own idea or if he was prompted by Quinny's not-so-subtle suggestion. Either way, it's nice of him. I watch Foster for a few seconds as he starts back along the road.

Dean comes up behind me and puts his arms around my waist. He leans in close and kisses my neck.

"Just a sec," I say and start to slide the window pane closed. Foster is up the winding campsite road now, a small distant figure, almost completely covered by darkness and out of sight.

But then something else is there.

It's the white buck.

I mean Speckles. Except this time he seems to be pure glowing light all on his own — a shiny, milky frozen white without a single shadow across him hiding or disguising anything. His illumination seems far too bright to be dismissed as a reflection of moonlight. His massive antlers seem to glow as well. He can't be more than ten feet behind Foster, and I know he wasn't there a second ago. How can Foster not sense him, hear him? The deer's taking the same path as if following him home.

Dean gives me another kiss on my neck.

"Dean, wait," I whisper. "Something's out there."

"What, is it Quinny again?"

I step to the side so he has to let go of me. The buck has paused near a cedar tree.

"No laugh for that?" Dean says.

"Look," I say and tap the glass in the direction of the deer. "Up there. I don't know what it's doing down here." I turn to Dean. He's still behind me and hasn't moved close enough to the window to see out.

"What's what doing?" Dean asks. "What are you talking about, Vi?"

I look back and it's still there. The buck lifts its head and turns towards me. Its eyes are pink — red really — as if glowing in headlights on the highway. Even from this distance its stare is so intense it gives me a chill. I wonder if Dean can feel how I've cooled. The beer that's floating on top of the wine in my stomach seems to swish and swirl.

"A buck. Come closer. Do you see him there?" I say it slow and clear as if I'm speaking to a child.

He looks out. "Where?"

"There." I tap the glass. I want him to say yes, need him to say, Yes, oh that white one, that's Speckles who Bliss used to talk about right, of course, sorry I was teasing.

"Vi, where? A deer? What's the big deal?"

He has to be able to see it. But I look back out and it's gone.

I don't answer Dean and rush straight outside. The screen door slams behind me and I jump down the two porch steps. I run around the corner of the cottage. Nothing. Then I head up the road, stop where the deer had been and look down for prints. It's too dark to tell without bending, rubbing my hand across the ground.

Dean is right behind me.

"Vi, holy liftin' what's up? Just how many drinks have you had?"

He touches my arm.

I take a step sideways to move out of his reach.

"A deer? Really? What's the difference? Has Dwayne been having a problem with them or something?"

I pause. "It's nothing."

"Really? It doesn't seem like nothing. You sure?"

"Yeah, it's fine."

"Well come back inside then, okay?"

I take a quick final look around before we head in. No buck anywhere.

Dean goes straight to the bedroom, but I stop first in the living room and sit on the couch. I leave the light off. I concentrate on deliberately taking a breath in through my nose and blowing it out through my mouth. That was Speckles again, same as last time. Except the antlers? No, it was Speckles with his crazy antlers. And of course he wasn't glowing. A large part of Speckles is white, far more of him is white than brown — his coat is like a lightly toasted marshmallow. If he was standing so his spots were in shadow, he very well could look like a ghostly buck. If there was such a thing. I mean, if Speckles dressed up for Halloween it would be an easy costume for him. Dean was right, I had more than plenty to drink, and I let my imagination go a little wilder than it would sober. It was Speckles I saw. Done.

Dean comes out of the bedroom.

"You coming in?" he asks. "Or are you waiting for him to come back?" A careful grin.

I get up.

"No." I shake my head. I know it's best to believe he's not coming back.

10

I came close to returning to the boneyard the night that Bliss and I somehow convinced our parents to let us have a back-to-school party in the field behind the barn. At least half the high school came. Everybody brought tents to camp in and there was a bonfire. It had the makings of a legendary event — the kind of party that, years from now, everyone wants to claim they were at. Of course my father had conditions for us to abide by. Some were absolutes, some were bendable rules and some were easily ignored suggestions. We were not to start a forest fire. We were not to go in and trash the barn (we were allowed to go in the back door to the washrooms, but no further). No taking anything out of the barn; no Victorian settees or high back rockers getting dragged out to the field for campfire seating. No climbing on the roof of the barn. No evidence of drinking left behind. No breaking glass. No throwing up in the barn parking lot. No going near the highway. Pick up every bit of garbage. Be sure the campfire is put out. Everyone stays for the night and leaves in the morning sober.

But his most emphasized condition of all: no going anywhere near the woods. "For Christ's sake," my father said, "you keep those kids out of the damn woods. There's no way in hell I'm coming over here in the middle of the night and searching the forest for one of your friends." He looked from Bliss to me to Bliss again.

"Anybody gets drunk and stumbles out of the field and into the treeline, they can curl up on some moss and sleep it off until morning. I don't care if fifty Christly ghost deer come and dance on their head. You're old enough to take care of yourselves."

"It's cool, Dad, don't worry. Really," Bliss said. "We'll have it set up so good no one will want to go anywhere else."

My father looked straight at him and nodded. He'd said what he wanted to say.

Bliss and I got to work. The timothy and other grasses in the field were thigh-high and we had to clear an area to use. It was well beyond anything that could be tamed with a lawn mower, so we took advantage of the fact that the barn was basically a vintage department and hardware store. Bliss got a huge scythe and I found a little sickle. My father sharpened them with a stone until the blades shone bright. Bliss walked ahead of me through the tall grass with the scythe straight up above his shoulder like the grim reaper. The sun went under one of the few clouds and he turned quickly and tried to give me an evil look like something out of a horror movie, as he pretended to trace his finger along the blade. I had to laugh. I didn't end up doing much with my dinky sickle because Bliss was so good with the scythe. He had a giant area finished in no time. I took an old hay rake from the barn and cleared what he had cut.

We made a fire pit. For the bottom we took some big rocks from the stream, and while we were at it Bliss left three apples, which he claimed were "party food" for Speckles. Together we hauled back all the barn's picnic tables. We put up our family tent and unfolded the six lawn chairs we'd taken from the deck at home. Bliss looked around when we were done, surveying the whole scene and smiling as if we'd planted a garden or something.

"So can you dig it, Vi?" he asked. "I've got a really good feeling about this." He nodded several times.

"Yeah," I said. "Me too." How could I not? It wasn't every day that Bliss said he had a really good feeling about something.

People started showing up at nine, just as it was getting dark. Dean came, and Barkley and Jill and Johnny. Plus about a hundred other people. Barkley brought a ridiculously huge family tent with three sets of poles that all had to be angled perfectly, so it was a tangled trap waiting to collapse. Bliss got the campfire roaring right off. He'd gathered a huge pile of dead wood and fallen branches from the forest and bought four bundles of kindling and camp wood from Seven Birches. People gathered near the fire in little groups and around the picnic tables and chairs. Music was playing from an eight-track player set on the tailgate of our truck and plugged into the barn with three long extension cords. Johnny was in charge of the tunes and brought more tapes than he could ever play. The music was good. And loud. Loud enough to drown out the sound of the highway traffic. Fireflies were blinking in the field. You could smell the woodsmoke in the air and still feel the warmth of the day hovering in the night. People were talking, drinking, singing, laughing, some were dancing.

Everything was going great until Suzy Gibbons decided to pee in the woods. She was a girl in junior high who had tagged along with her older sister Connie and was drinking for the first time. No one missed her at first, but when Connie clued in that she hadn't seen her in a while, and asked around, she figured out it had been a good half-hour since Suzy had gone past the treeline.

Jill and I were sitting on a picnic table when Connie rushed over to us. We'd been singing along at the top of our lungs to every song Johnny was playing.

"Violet, oh my God, you have to get Suzy! She went in the woods and no one's seen her. Mom's gonna kill me. You have to go get her. Please. You have to! And Bliss. Take Bliss. He can find her!" Then she started crying.

Jill, pretty much because Connie's next move was to collapse into her, hugged her and smoothed her hair like she was a baby. "Don't worry," Jill said, making Connie cry even louder. "It's not your fault. Don't worry, really. We'll get her." Jill raised her eyebrows at me.

I had no desire to go anywhere near the woods at that moment. I felt like telling Connie Gibbons that no one had invited a little kid to the party, let alone suggested giving her drinks. And why on Earth couldn't she have used a real washroom with a flush and running water that I'd begged my father to let us have access to — a special privilege no one else hosting a field party would have ever been able to provide.

Across the field I could see Bliss and Barkley and Dean. They had made some sort of toast and clinked their beer bottles together. Then one of them must have said something hilarious because all three laughed and laughed. Bliss was so happy. He was having such a good time. But here was Connie, upset and crying. A sister's worry. I had no choice.

I jumped off the picnic table. "Okay girls, let's go round up some recruits. Goodbye field party. Hello search party." I think I sounded enthusiastic. "Don't worry, Connie, we'll find her," I added.

"Yeah, come on," Jill said. Jill grabbed her flashlight, the only one between the three of us, and we headed across the field towards the campfire.

"So there's the future Mrs. Saunderson," Dean said. "I was wondering where you went."

Bliss rolled his eyes. Dean and I weren't boyfriend and girlfriend yet. And it was easy to be silly when we were all together back then.

I told Bliss and Dean about Suzy. The fire let out a pop and a spray of sparks flew from the pit as if to add a dramatic flourish.

Bliss tilted his head way back and stared up at the sky. Then he dropped his chin low to his chest. I felt awful for wrecking his fun. Because drinking or not, we both knew.

It's easy enough to get lost in unfamiliar woods in the middle of a sunny day without a drop of alcohol in your system. Even experienced hunters sometimes get lost in our New Brunswick forest. As soon as you're far enough along that you lose sight of where you came in, it's easy to get turned around. It all looks the same. Trees ahead of you and behind you, left and right. Time stretches out. Seconds seem like minutes and minutes, hours. Panic comes long before it should.

"Five minutes," Bliss said. "Don't leave the field, but check every tent and ask everybody and then come right back here. And Vi, can you check the barn?"

I so wished she'd been in there, making out with someone, getting felt up on an old oak church pew. But she wasn't anywhere, except probably tripping through the dark forest getting her hair tangled with twigs, snagging and wrecking the new top she'd bought for the party — hopefully not so far in that we wouldn't be able to come across her.

"Okay," Bliss said when we'd all arrived back at the fire. "Barkley, you're still pretty much sober, right? You're coming with me. Everybody else stays here. Violet, you be sure that no one else comes in after us."

"Hey Bliss," Dean said. "I'm coming too. You best not leave me unattended around your foxy sister." He winked at me.

"Jesus, Dean, this isn't a joke," Bliss said.

"Shit, Bliss, calm it down. Holy liftin'," Dean said. "I'm coming to help that's all. The more people looking, the more chance we have of getting her." Dean stepped towards Bliss and put his hand on his shoulder. He looked right at him.

"Okay, sorry, man, we're cool," Bliss said.

"He's right. We're coming too," I said. I wanted to get this over with as quickly as possible, and I also wasn't interested in playing everyone's babysitter.

I walked across the meadow with Jill beside me, shining her flashlight in front of us. Connie came along, but as soon as we stepped into the trees, she broke down crying again so I suggested Jill take her back. I took the flashlight. Dean caught up to me. Barkley and Bliss weren't far behind.

"Dean and I will follow the stream," I said. "You guys go on the other side, along the edge a ways before you start in?" I made it sound like a question.

"Be careful, Vi," Bliss said.

And so we went. Beyond the first branches.

It was pitch-dark in the woods. It was as if the land we were walking towards hadn't been created yet. A black abyss. The moon was almost full, and it was a clear night with a million stars. But only the slightest moonlight was coming through the break in the trees for the stream, subtly reflecting on the water. I gave Dean the flashlight to carry and held his other hand. He wrapped his fingers in between mine, and in any other situation I would have dwelt on how nice it felt. We moved ahead in the dark. The water in the stream was gurgling, and we could hear our every step. Nothing else was moving. All of nature seemed to be sleeping. Or perhaps listening, waiting quietly to see how this would all turn out.

"Suzy," I yelled. "Suzy!" Dean called for her as well. Bliss and Barkley repeated her name again and again in the distance. Dean and I started carefully walking up the side of the stream. Yelling then listening. I could tell I was squeezing Dean's hand. The flashlight really didn't make that wide a path.

I tripped on a raised root and fell. I almost pulled Dean down with me, but he only toppled sideways.

"Tree grab you, did it?" he asked.

We both laughed. It made me feel better.

I got up and we walked on with Dean guiding me. I was feeling the drinks I'd had, and that, along with hardly being able to see anything in front of me, was a bad combination. I stumbled on some moss near the stream edge, but Dean kept me from slipping into the water. That was funny too. Then when I tripped for the third time, maybe on a fallen branch, I did take Dean down with me.

I lay flat on the forest floor, staring up through the dark fringe of leaves to the specks of distant starlight in a black sky. Dean stayed beside me, still holding my hand, and then he ever so gently kissed me on the cheek. I turned to him and he kissed me again, longer, and I completely forgot about the fact that I was on the cold damp ground in the woods with bits of moss and rusty dried pine needles stuck to me. It was the first time we kissed.

But in a minute we each rolled back flat on the forest floor and stared at the night sky.

"That was nice," he said.

"Yeah."

We didn't move. He held my hand and time passed.

I lay still, waiting, hoping that he'd kiss me again, but the longer we stayed quiet, the more awkward the silence became.

"We should probably get up," I finally said. "Wouldn't want to get trampled by the ghost herd if they decide to run by this way." I laughed. I was joking and hoped that Dean might laugh too. But he didn't.

"You believe in all that?" he asked.

"What? Ghost deer? Highly unlikely. The boneyard's real though, I've seen it. And actually it's not that far from here if you'd like a guided tour."

"Really?" Dean asked. He didn't laugh that time either.

I should have known enough to leave it alone. It was so stupid of me to suggest. I was trying too hard, chattering to break the uncomfortable silence.

But Dean was instantly curious. "Is it far? Can we go?" he asked.

It was too late to say I was kidding and take it back. I could hear in his voice how much he wanted to go. Plus he'd just kissed me, and I didn't want to disappoint him and wreck everything.

"We'll see," I said. "Maybe Suzy wandered there anyway."

We stood and I reached again for Dean's hand. I took the flashlight and shone it all around trying to orient myself. The beam lit tree trunks, a fallen log, ferns, underbrush, the stream, brown dead leaves blown into a clump against a giant moss-covered rock.

We weren't that far. Even though I stayed away from the place, I never forgot how to get there. Every detail of the whole scene from the first and only time I went with Bliss was clear in my mind. I could play it through in slow motion and look for the subtle landmarks to guide me. We were already in the forest in the darkness of night, searching for a lost drunk girl. Surely some old inanimate bones lying in a pile somewhere weren't going to make the situation much worse.

I shone the flashlight up the stream, making the ripples sparkle.

"Suzy!" I yelled.

"Suzy!" Dean yelled too.

I was more sure-footed then, determined and stepping carefully, holding Dean's hand. I watched for a dead log across the whole width of the water and then two pointy rocks side by side sticking up on the far edge of the stream. We turned into the forest and cut across the slight slope that led to the boneyard. We kept yelling for Suzy, the sound of her name dissipating again and again into distant trees.

We stepped over underbrush and pushed low branches out of the way, being careful that they didn't hit either of us when they sprang back in retaliation. We walked around clumps of ferns and past a decaying log. Soon enough, under the bright circle of the flashlight, was a bone glowing white.

Ahead of us was the place that the trees stop and the carcasses begin. The clearing for the giant pit let the moonlight through, a beam from the sky. I could already smell the rot: meat gone bad. A little bit of the metallic smell of blood mixed with rancid cheese.

"You go on — if you want," I told Dean and handed him the flashlight. "But you know, you don't have to. I'm not." I looked right at him. "It's kind of gross." Understatement of the year.

"I'll just be a second," Dean said.

Meanwhile I stood alone in the forest in the pitch-dark.

And he wasn't just gone a second. He went to the edge of the pit and stopped. I could see the beam of the flashlight moving back and forth.

The longer he stood and I waited, the creepier I started to feel. I reminded myself of all the times I'd told Bliss not to magnify the meaning of the boneyard, to resist twisting his memory of it into a big deal. And I knew far better than to let my mind wander back to childhood stories of ghost deer coming out at night. I knew better than to spook myself. But it was as if the place gave off more than a smell. It gave off a vibe. It was not a good place to be standing near, by yourself, ever — let alone at night. My mouth went dry, and I ran my tongue all over my teeth. I felt a tightening in my chest.

"Dean," I called. It made me even more nervous to hear the uncertainty in my voice. "Let's go."

No response.

I was definitely starting to freak myself out. I knew I was being ridiculous. It really was black-hole dark without the flashlight though. And I swore I could suddenly feel someone, something, behind me, watching.

"Dean!" I yelled again. Finally I could see the flashlight beam stop moving around — as if he was finished looking.

I tried to stay calm and I reminded myself that it would only be a matter of seconds until Dean returned to me. But then I heard footsteps coming from the opposite direction. I know I did. Twigs on the ground were snapping. Dried-out leaves were getting crunched. By hooves? There seemed to be a pale light behind me, as though a translucent form was approaching. I didn't dare turn around, but I was positive something was there. Getting closer. I heard my name. It wasn't Dean who said it, and I screamed.

It woke the crows who were sleeping in the trees near the boneyard and there was an insanely loud sound — as intense as thunder directly overhead — of the birds cawing, their wings flapping, branches shifting and scraping against each other. It sent a chill over me.

"Christ," I finally heard, and I spun around to see Foster holding a torch. "Violet, you trying to wake the dead?"

Dean rushed over and pulled me back. I sagged into him.

"What are you doing out here?" Dean asked Foster.

"I think that'd be a better question for you."

"You pretty much gave me three heart attacks, Foster," I managed to say. I could tell my fingernails were digging into Dean and I loosened my grip. "Do you always wander around out here at night?"

"Only when I hear something. Come on," he said, "I'm pretty damn sure I know why you're out here anyway."

"I doubt it," I replied. "This really wasn't a planned trip."

"Suit yourself," Foster said. "But for now don't move, and Violet, brace yourself, this is going to be loud."

He stepped ahead and lowered his torch. He stabbed the unlit end of it into the ground. A trap sprung and snapped, lurching from under the dead leaves. It jumped and bit with such force that splinters flew from the wood. We had been within feet of crippling ourselves with it.

"Jesus," Dean said.

Foster picked up the chain from the trap and looped it over his arm.

Then without a word he turned and walked not more than thirty paces into the forest. I thought maybe he was leaving but he stopped. Lowered his torch.

There was Suzy passed out, curled up at the base of a tree. She was obviously really far gone if none of the noise we'd just caused had woken her.

"She's one of yours, I take it," he said.

We should have thanked Foster, but he was gone in a second. We went to Suzy and with a lot of shaking and coaxing, and finally dragging her to the stream and splashing water on her face, we were able to rouse her.

Suzy was so wasted. She had no idea how close she'd been to waking up hungover and cold in the forest, with a squirrel playing in her hair. And then likely being grounded for a year. As we dragged her, she stumbled back and forth between Dean and me. She kept singing "Row, row, row your boat" over and over like she couldn't remember any more words but was vaguely aware it had something to do with the nearby stream.

Bliss and Barkley were already back at the forest's edge and must have heard us coming because they walked in to meet us. Bliss shone his flashlight in our direction and when it passed over Suzy's face, she switched from singing "Row, row, row" to "Here comes the sun," then giggled like she was hilarious. I couldn't get rid of her a second too soon. The walk back had taken almost an hour. One of my feet was soaked from the stream. I hadn't been able to talk to Dean at all since we found her, and her whiny drunken singing was driving me batty.

But the relief and then happiness on Bliss's face was worth it.

"You got her, thank God. You totally saved our asses," he said. "Here, you guys must be tired." Bliss came over to switch with me, and Barkley headed for Dean's side. Suzy looked small between them. She leaned against Barkley and closed her eyes.

"So where was she?" Barkley asked.

"Way, way back," I said.

"Almost at the—" Dean started.

"Near Foster's place," I interrupted.

Dean glanced at me.

"He found her first," I continued. "We owe him one."

"I owe you one, Vi," Bliss said.

Dean loudly cleared his throat. "Ahem," he said.

Bliss turned to him. "You too, good buddy. Or how about this then? Right here, future Mrs. Saunderson," Bliss nodded his head in my direction. "With my blessing."

"Well now," Dean said. "There's a reward and a half."

"You may kiss the bride," Bliss announced as if he was a wedding officiant.

Dean licked his lips.

Bliss raised his arm across his face. "As long as I'm not around to see it," he said and laughed.

I probably should have protested, but all I could do was roll my eyes.

"This calls for a celebration drink!" Barkley announced.

We all walked out of the forest.

With the end of summer and the start of school, it was the middle of September before Dean and I were alone again. One Saturday afternoon Dean came to our place to play basketball with Bliss. Barkley and Johnny had been there earlier but left to go stalk the liquor store parking lot to see who they could convince to buy them beer. I was inside watching TV, pretending to ignore them, when my father pulled the truck across the end of the driveway.

He'd come from the store. He had a big oak sideboard in the back of the truck that someone from Riverbend had bought. Dad needed Bliss to help with the delivery and promised it wouldn't take more than twenty minutes. Dean volunteered to go too, but my father had a bunch of other stuff piled in the cab so there was no room. Dad told him to go inside and joked that maybe I'd serve him some lemonade. Mom was at the store for the day.

"Yeah," Bliss said. "Go on in and woo Vi. Just don't run off and elope or anything before I get back."

Dean knocked before he came in and called for me, even though he knew exactly where I was, because our eyes had met a few times as he ran by the window.

"So you want some lemonade?" I asked.

We ended up sitting together on the couch, not quite side by side but more end to end. There was silence at first, which was ridiculous. We spoke all the time, even if usually there were other people around.

I thought maybe he'd inch closer and make a move, and I figured I'd let him, but instead he started talking.

"Hey, you know that night at the party? That night we went to the boneyard? I never did tell Bliss."

"About us? Yeah," I said. "I know, me neither."

"Well, that." He smiled a little, although he also might have looked slightly embarrassed. "But about seeing the boneyard, I mean. You cut me off when I was going to mention it and I thought there must have been a reason."

"Just gross, that's all. Didn't need to wreck the party mood any more than it already had been."

Dean nodded. "Fair enough." He shrugged and didn't seem to think anything more of it. He didn't know I was lying.

The truth was that I had no intention of ever mentioning the boneyard to Bliss again in his life — unless he brought it up first. Bliss hadn't talked to me about it in a long time, not since the day, years before, when we saw the dead buck at the grocery store parking lot. But I knew it was still there, thriving in his mind, as much as he tried to keep it buried. And over time, witnessing what he struggled with had gradually changed my memory of the day we first saw the boneyard too. What I remember most, what stands out more than anything, is Bliss pulling me back, trying to stop me from seeing it.

I wish it had been the other way around. I wish I'd been the one to protect Bliss.

That is my altered recollection, my haunting thought — really my ultimate regret — about seeing the boneyard. Because I know it's far too late for me to shield Bliss from his memory of it now.

Dean nodded and took a drink of his lemonade.

I took a sip from my glass as well.

"But you know," Dean said, "you were right before. I didn't say anything to him about us either."

"Oh yeah?"

"But I've actually thought a lot about it. A whole lot. It was nice."

I looked down at the couch. "Yeah, it was," I said.

"Just maybe not in the woods next time," Dean said.

He set his glass of lemonade on the coffee table and shifted a little closer to me on the couch.

I inched over a bit too, and he reached for my hand.

The front door opened.

"I'm back!" It was Bliss.

And at the time I was so annoyed that he had interrupted us. But now I'd love more than anything for him to come through the door.

11

Foster is sitting at a picnic table when I pull in the parking lot at nine, even though we aren't going to the Vaughn cottage until ten. He nods as I drive past. I park the truck behind the barn and head around front. Dean's mowing the playground area. I wave and wait until he waves back. I was awake before he left this morning, but I didn't let on as he quietly got ready and tiptoed out.

It's a sunny, bright day again with the slightest breeze coming up from the river. I catch a whiff of Foster. It's Aqua Velva, half the bottle at least, but an older, skunkier version, as if he only uses it once a year — or decade. His hair is neatly combed and parted. His beard is trimmed. And his clothes — a plaid shirt and jeans — look clean and even pressed. He could easily be mistaken for a local or tourist. His old scuffed work boots are a bit out of place and perhaps a giveaway, but that's it.

"Violet," he says, "I'm at your service."

"Hey Foster, thanks, but we can't go for quite a while yet."

"I'll be here." I wait, but he doesn't say anything else. There's a book beside him on the picnic table. I shrug and go inside. Maybe he'll air out a bit in the meantime.

. . .

Our first customer of the day is already in the barn, looking through a box labelled "Instant Ancestors." Dad sometimes ends up with old photos from estates — ancient, posed shots of long-forgotten relatives. Some of the pictures are metal tintypes and some are cabinet cards made of stiff cardboard. It's rare that either type has a name written on them, so no one knows who the people in the photos are anymore. Dad puts all the unidentified pictures in the same box, for the bargain price of twenty-five cents an *ancestor*. (Or mix and match a whole made-up family for the deal of five for a dollar.) Pretty funny if you ask me, but of course Quinny thinks the idea is disrespectful and that it offends more customers than it entertains. The photos sell nonetheless.

Elizabeth agreed to come early today since it's Saturday and it'll be busy, and I have no idea how long I'll be gone. She is dusting furniture at the far end of the barn and she waves at me when I come in.

Quinny has a new quilt draped over her arm — nothing intricate this time but still pretty, patchwork squares in mint-green fabrics. She's looking up at the beams in the ceiling and acknowledges me only with a shift of her eyes.

"You see how spiffed-up Foster looks?" I ask. "You see him outside?"

"I believe I smelled him," she says, still looking upward. "All that aftershave has to be an attempt to cover some other foul stench."

"He was down showering at the campsite last night. He's really taking all this very seriously. I think Dad —"

"Violet, will you hold the ladder while I hang this, please?"

She can't stand even talking about it. The very thought of Foster and me going down to the Vaughn place today is eating away at her. Maybe I'll be nice and choose something from the house to give her as a little memento — depending on what's there. It might be enough to keep her from driving me crazy with digging for more details. If she wasn't so fundamentally repulsed by Foster I'm sure she'd be out there working on him. Telling him to keep his eyes peeled the whole time, to make mental notes of every detail and to come straight to her with a full report.

I move things around the store — touching, shifting small items like vases and bowls from shelf to table — until it's time to leave. Then I find Dean in the parking lot.

"So listen," I start. "About last night —"

"I mentioned it to Dwayne," Dean says. "Don't worry about it."

"To Dwayne?"

"I went to the canteen this morning, and I told him you thought there was a deer bothering stuff in the campground last night. He said no one else said anything — and he didn't see what a deer could hurt anyway — but to let him know if you see it again."

"Okay."

"But between you and me, Vi, a deer? Really? What's the difference?"

I step aside so a car can pull into a parking spot and don't respond right away.

"Or wait, no!" Dean says. "Of course, how could I forget?" He raises his arms above his head and begins to sway back and forth in a completely disjointed way, a disco dance disaster. "Was it another ghoooooossssttt deeeeer? Ooooooooh."

I look towards Foster who's still at the picnic table. He's watching Dean too but goes back to reading when our eyes meet.

"Nice," I say.

"What, not even a smile? Ooooooooooh." Dean's still waving his arms around. He looks ridiculous and the customers getting out of the car are staring. But I know he's doing it for me.

"Okay, enough," I say and smile. "Now quit it before you dislocate your shoulder or something."

He lowers his arms. Shrugs. Rolls his shoulders. "Seems okay," he says. "Listen, Vi. I know you're off since your parents left. But last night? Sure, you weren't exactly sober but you seemed really worked up. So do you want to clue me in?"

I look down. Over to Foster. He's still reading his book.

"No need to worry." I hug Dean and he kisses me on the cheek. "Really," I say. "Unless you want to worry about me messing up the Vaughn estate deal. There's always that."

"Never." He steps back and looks directly at me, his hands on my shoulders. "You got it, Vi. You're an antiques superstar. Now scram."

Foster and I leave right at ten as planned. I have two thousand dollars cash locked in the dash of the truck. That's the amount the Vaughns asked for. (And knowing that in itself is a huge relief. I don't have to come up with an offer, which is often the case.) Foster has his window rolled all the way down. His book is on the seat beside him. It's *Under Sealed Orders* by H.A. Cody. Foster's watching the scenery go by.

"You really don't get out for a drive much, do you?" I say.

He shakes his head. "Over to town for food once in a while. Your father'll take me or I'll hitchhike. That's it."

"When was the last time you drove yourself?"

He thinks for a moment. "Late sixties."

"This is 1977."

He lifts his wrist as if looking at an imaginary watch. "Is it now?"

"Do you miss it?"

"Miss what? Driving around?"

All of it is what I'd like to say — being a part of regular society, living near other people, not having to hitchhike for groceries, not having to walk through the woods in the middle of the night to take a shower in a public washroom at a campsite.

"No," he answers anyway.

We're silent after that. The sun is bright so I flip down the visor. We're driving slow in a long line of traffic. A boy and a girl in the car in front of us are turned around looking back. They pop their heads up and down. Foster waves. I wonder if the kids could ever guess how it is we were thrown together, where we're going and why.

Down the highway we pass the access road to the boneyard, then after another mile or so we go through Holy Hollow, which is the nickname for the mini valley where there are two churches and a church hall. A transport truck has been tailgating us, waiting for a chance to get by, although no one in front of us is going any faster. There are hardly any passing lanes and some of those are suicide lanes anyway — marked so cars from either direction can pull out. Using them is a dangerous guessing game and I've never dared try one, although Bliss and Dad sometimes would. We finally turn onto Pine Lake Road and drive away from the highway, up a hill and then down again towards the lake.

At the end of the road there's a big parking lot, public beach and canteen. Behind the canteen is a little campground. Those things are on the right, but we turn left onto a bumpy dirt road that winds behind the cottages. The road is shadowed by overhanging branches and a few low ones ping the windshield. I try my best to avoid the deep ruts in the road, but if we buy anything fragile I'm going to have to bundle it enough to survive being dropped from Mars so it arrives at the barn in one piece.

We gradually round the side of the lake and come to a fork in the road. The driveway to the Vaughns' cottage is marked by two old grey cedar posts. There's a rusty chain unhooked and coiled on the ground near one of them. The road beyond it is covered with green — weeds and grass, and flowers like buttercups, daisies, and Queen Anne's lace. But there are tire tracks where these plants have been squished down.

I drive ahead and it's a steady rhythm — *ping, ping, ding, ding* under the truck, *thwackety-tick-tack* of low branches on the windshield. A rabbit bounds across the road in front of us. We shake and bump and thump until finally there's a curve, and we come into a small clearing. Tall grass has been cut back and is laying around drying out. A man is smoking, leaning against a green truck. It's the caretaker, Cecil, an old guy with grey hair tufting out on each side of his Irving ball cap. His face is red with sunburn. He's wearing a blue plaid shirt with jeans and work boots. He sees us and waves.

"So here we go," I say to Foster. And although it crossed my mind earlier to suggest that Foster wait in the truck, I'm not going to. He's hard to read, but he's had a subtle smile on his face the whole time; I think he might be enjoying himself.

I wait a bit before I get out. I know the energy surge that my father can feel, the rush, the thrill of the hunt; it's the little squeeze of anxiety I feel around my rib cage now. I mean, I understand completely. It's uncharted territory out here. I need this estate. Need it — for Dad and for The Purple Barn. I have to be friendly and businesslike. I have to seem trustworthy, confident, as if I've done this a hundred times before. I so hope it's not all mouse-chewed junky furniture, chipped china and Melmac dishes, partially unravelled afghans and beat-up rusty cutlery. This place has a reputation to live up to.

"Violet," Foster says, "your father wouldn't have sent you if he wasn't sure you could handle it."

"Thanks, Foster."

We get out. It's a little cooler here than at the barn. I can see the lake again and a walking path through the trees on the other side of the clearing.

"Miss Davis, glad you could come," Cecil says as he walks towards us. "Mr. Vaughn's not here yet, but I'll take you on in and let you start your look-see. And Mr. Kensey?" He extends his hand to Foster and they shake.

"Yes, Mr. Kensey," I say. "And please, call me Violet."

"Good enough, then," Cecil says. "I think you're going to be in for a pretty good surprise. It's all grown up out here, but inside it's the same as the day they left."

We start along the path through the little patch of woods — Cecil, me, then Foster. We walk maybe forty or fifty feet, along a sharp diagonal, and when we finally step from the trees we're facing the front of the cottage. It's a Cape Cod style house, white with black trim and two gables in the roof. There is what looks like a glassed-in sun porch on the side farthest away from us. The paint is peeling, but the building is straight and I don't see any shingles missing from the roof.

"It's not boarded up," I say.

"Had to take 'em all off once I knew they wanted the place cleaned out," Cecil explains. "There's been no power in there for years and it'd be pitch-black inside with the boards up. I'll take you in and you look around wherever, doesn't matter. Don't be shy. I don't know much about any antiques, but I see lots of stuff in there looks like something woulda been in my old gram's place, so I figure some'll be right what you want. Or it'll all be, I guess. Mr. Vaughn said to remind you he wants it all gone — all or none — doesn't want to be dragging a whole parade through here picking away at it bit by bit. But you've got first dibs on account of I put in a good word for your father."

I smile. "I appreciate that."

Cecil leads us to the house. As we get very close to the front step, which is made of two long slabs of pink granite, I realize we're walking over an old overgrown flat rock pathway. Weeds are covering it but I can feel it solid beneath my feet. Someone has started taming and trimming the giant rose bushes on each side of the path as well as the shrubs that line the front of the house. The place must have been gorgeous at one time. The door is a six-panel, painted a rich blue. There's a screen door in front of it with holes and pulls, but the wood in each corner is scrolled and ornate, like the trim on the frame of an important family picture.

Cecil takes out a key and unlocks the door. He lunges against it with his shoulder and it comes open.

"After you," he says.

I go in and Foster follows.

We step into an open space. It's unexpected, since older places like this are usually divided up into many smaller rooms. There are partial walls and a centre angled staircase with a landing. To the far left in the middle of the side wall is a stone fireplace made with smooth rocks and a thick pine mantel.

There's a huge dining-room set with twelve matched rabbit-eared pressback chairs in a dark stain, a sideboard, two cabinets and a serving stand. There are prints and paintings all over the walls and pewter plates and goblets lining the mantel.

"Pretty impressive, isn't it?" Cecil asks.

I slowly nod.

"Real nice lookin' old place," Foster says.

"Well you have your look-see, and I'll run down and see if Mr. Vaughn's come through yet."

He leaves and as soon as the screen door slams, Foster walks over to a glassed-in bookcase without saying a word.

I can smell the old wood in the house — the stale odour of it drying out over years. There is dust floating through the sunbeam coming in the window. Out of the corner of my eye I see Cecil heading back to the path outside. I'm going to look at as much as I can before he comes back.

The chairs in the sitting area include a small nursing rocker, a tall ladderback rocker and two more pressback side chairs. There are spaces where other seats may have been but I bet Cecil took out anything upholstered to prevent mice and squirrel's nest problems. I count four plant stands and three little side tables.

In the kitchen Foster is sitting and flipping through a book. I open the pantry cupboard door, and the inside is packed. There are dishes:

stacks of blue willow pieces, countless bone china cups and saucers, a copper lustre sugar bowl, an old glass rolling pin, a marigold carnival glass vase squeezed in the back, a flow blue covered vegetable serving dish, along with several pieces of Royal Bayreuth china (which makes me think of the time a customer misheard Dad and excitedly asked, "That china belonged to Babe Ruth?"). There's another jelly cupboard built into the wall, and with a quick peek I can see that it's crammed full of beautiful china too.

I go upstairs and quickly walk through the first three bedrooms. Each has an antique bed: one cast iron and painted a crisp white, one brass and one a spool bed. Each room also has a dresser; two are either walnut or mahogany, but one is flame birch. There are more prints on the walls, a toy model ship in one room, two more rocking chairs, a plant stand, a music stand being used as a night table, an ironstone bowl and pitcher set on a maple commode.

Then in the last bedroom is a beautiful cottage-pine stencilled bedroom set. The pine is painted a faint buttery yellow and the sten-cilling — scrolls, flowers and birds — is done in three shades of brown with red highlights. I'm at the foot of the bed when I hear the front door open and close. Then Cecil's voice.

Dad will be thrilled. I am buying it all, just like Mr. Vaughn asked. All I have to do is politely communicate that to him. And he's in the house now. Waiting.

Downstairs, Cecil is in the kitchen, but there's only a woman with him. She's heavy-set and flushed. Her long greyish brown hair is mostly pulled up in a bun, but there are a mess of strands loose. Many are stuck with sweat to her neck. She's sitting near Foster, leaning ahead against the table, looking down and breathing heavily. There's a long, dark red, fresh-looking scratch on her right arm.

"Violet, this is my wife, Mavis," Cecil says when he sees me at the base of the stairs. "It seems Mr. Vaughn called not more than a minute after I was down the driveway."

"Violet, nice to meet you. But now first thing, dear, please excuse my appearance," Mavis says, smoothing her hair. "Goodness, I didn't dare bring the car down that mess of a road — if that's what you can even call it — so I had to walk in." She stops to take a deep breath. "And I must, say, Lordy, that was quite a trek."

"Well I certainly appreciate you coming out with the message," I say. "So Mr. Vaughn won't be here today?"

Cecil answers. "Apparently he finally heard from a lawyer in Fredericton who he's been after forever. Wants to talk to him about selling the place and he didn't want to miss the chance meeting with him — really, really hard fellow to get a hold of I guess. He sends his apologies."

"He's selling the cottage?" I ask.

"Cottage and all the land as far as I know."

"Did he say when he'd be able to come here again? Or leave a way to get a hold of him?"

"Can't say he did, dear," Mavis says. "But he did say he'd call Cecil here later." She looks up at him. "And he did want me to be sure to apologize for your inconvenience."

"Well, tell him we understand, and that we're most absolutely interested. The entire contents just like he wants."

"For sure, Violet, I'll tell him," Cecil says.

"At his earliest opportunity," I say. I glance to Foster. "We'll be happy to come right out again." I hope I don't sound too needy, but now that I've seen the contents I feel even more anxious. We have to have this stuff.

"Must have been a nice way to live don't you think, Violet?" Mavis says. "Surrounded by all these wonderful things."

I nod.

"Goodness, just the best of everything. I really don't know that I could've just up and left. I know it was sad about the boy. A tragedy. But it's such a shame that they didn't come back. Time does heal. It's harder I'm sure that he was young, but —"

Foster loudly slides his chair. "Well, now, Violet —" he interrupts her. He looks at me.

Mavis stops talking and her face flushes again.

"Oh," Mavis says. "Oh, sorry, I do know you need to be going." Then she starts talking even more quickly than before. "But well now, Violet, I think that's so wonderful your parents had a chance to get away. They certainly deserve it. Good, good folks your mom and dad are. Everyone just thinks the best of them. Good, good people."

"Thanks," I say. "And it is a beautiful place. You're right. Lovely taste in everything."

Mavis smiles a little. "Yes, and Ivy's rainbow room, sakes alive, I've never seen such a thing. So special. To sit in there and have tea."

"Is it upstairs?" I ask.

"Oh! Oh, you didn't see it then. No, no, it's the sun porch. Oh dear, it would have been a shame to miss it. Oh my land. It won't take long. And you come too, Mr. Kensey." She turns to Foster who's still sitting at the table. "Or I should say Foster, you know." A twinkle in her eye. "I met you once when you were only a wee thing. Your mother was Dorothea, right? Lovely woman. God bless her soul."

Foster smiles. "That's kind of you to say."

"Well you must see this," Mavis says.

We follow her across the kitchen, and she opens the door to the sun porch. I go in first and then Foster.

The walls of the rainbow room are painted white. So is the wicker furniture. So are the dozens of skinny shelves — little ledges with no backs — set in front of every window lining three sides of the room. But on those shelves, arranged in groups by colour, is a collection of glassware like nothing I've ever seen before. Hundreds of pieces. There are bottles, little vases, toothpick holders, pin dishes, salt and pepper shakers, shot glasses, cordials and tumblers. There is a section of greenish-yellow Vaseline glass, one of pink and green Depression glass, marigold carnival glass, cranberry glass, a group of old cobalt-blue poison and perfume bottles and sun-tinted amethyst glass. Then across the windows at the front of the cottage, the ones facing the water, there is a huge collection of ruby glass.

Mavis steps into the sun porch behind us.

"Can you imagine the sun hitting all this just right? Later this afternoon it will be like magic in here."

"It's beautiful," I say. I walk along the windows, looking at all the glassware. Some of it is very old, and there are many pieces I don't think we've ever had in the store before.

When I reach the end with the ruby glass, Mavis joins me. The ruby-flashed crystal pieces are all souvenir items — toothpick holders shaped like buckets and hats and pots, little vases and tumblers — printed or engraved with place names. Years ago, pieces like this were sold in general stores in most communities so even the tiniest villages had a memento ready for purchase. I see Pokiok, Dumfries, Fredericton, Hawkshaw — some with words printed in gold, some with white, some engraved. But then in a section in the middle I see Haventon again and again. There are dozens, and some are marked with dates on the back. There is a sweet little canoe-shaped pin dish with "Souvenir of Haventon, NB" engraved on the front in a lacy script.

"Her hometown," Mavis says. "Ivy's. These were all hers from when the cottage was first built. She bought a few every summer. Souvenirs of good times. I think all year she looked forward to coming back here."

Mavis is right. This room does have a feeling, a warmth — only positive thoughts. There is no sadness of a drowned boy lingering in here. This is a place of happy memories established long before. I can't resist picking up and turning around several pieces, looking for the year on the back. I can already see them in The Purple Barn's Community Days booth on little glass shelves, maybe even with a mirror at the back and a floodlight shining on them. It would be our best display ever.

"Well you come back out when you're ready, dear," Mavis says and turns back to Foster. "So do you still like to read, Foster? You know I'm remembering now your mother telling me you were already going through big books by the time you started school."

I don't hear Foster's response as they have both walked back out to the kitchen. I stay only a couple of minutes longer. I know I shouldn't dwell.

Cecil is in the kitchen. "All set?" he asks.

"I am. But I was thinking, I could pay you now to save Mr. Vaughn the trouble of coming again later. I brought —"

"Oh, no, no," Cecil interrupts. "That's all right. You best not be giving me any opportunity to lose any money. And I'm sure Mr. Vaughn will want to meet you anyway."

"Okay, well, be sure to tell him I'll gladly come right back out at his earliest convenience." I can't help repeating myself. "Even if it's short notice. Call the barn and I'll come right down."

The highway is just as busy on the drive back. We wait a long time to turn out of the Pine Lake Road and then again to turn in at The Purple Barn. The parking lot is only about half full but there's a tour bus pulled diagonally across the end near the sign. Dean's outside and I beep at him.

"You know your boyfriend's got quite the dance moves," Foster says. It's the first time he's spoken since we left the cottage, and it takes me a few seconds to clue in to what he means. He saw Dean this morning waving his arms around like he needed to be rescued — his ghost deer imitation. Which is perfect because I've been waiting, wondering how I could bring up the topic, and now is my chance. I want to ask Foster if he noticed anything last night when he walked back from the campground. More specifically, did he see a deer tagging along behind him like a pet, following him home? Or maybe, hey, remember the last time you saw good old Speckles? What are his antlers looking like lately?

I just need to park the truck behind the barn. I grip the steering wheel tight in anticipation. I glance to Foster as I put the gear shift into park.

"Is he good to you, Violet?" Foster asks.

That was not a question I was expecting. "Dean?" I ask. Foster is watching me. "Yeah," I say. "He is."

Foster nods. "Good enough, then. Let me know when we're going to the lake again."

And in one motion it seems, he opens the truck door, hops out, slams it and is halfway across the meadow.

I missed my chance to ask. That quick. But I could easily catch up to him. Get moving. Now.

Or now.

I don't. I sit.

Because disbelieving can be every bit as hard as believing. I'll admit I don't dare ask Foster about the white buck because, deep down, I either already know the answer or else don't want to know.

Maybe it could make perfect sense that I'm being haunted.

Quinny sees me the instant I come through the front door of the barn. I'm sure she's been waiting for me, probably counting the seconds, but now that she knows I'm here, she pretends I'm not. She works away at the cash, carefully wrapping a large set of dishes in newspaper — piece by piece. She watches me go into the storage room, head down to the washroom — in then out — neaten a display of old handkerchiefs on a table and finally find Pepper Shaker.

Only then does she approach.

"Violet," she says, "you're back."

"I am," I say. Pepper Shaker hops out of my arms. He doesn't like Quinny. She never, ever pets him, and his black fur combined with his preference to sleep on anything soft and cozy is one of the reasons her quilts hang from the rafters.

"So did you bring any of the items back with you? Shall I go fetch Dean to unload your purchases?" she asks.

Fetch Dean. Right. I'm sure she's glanced out and knows the back of the truck is empty.

I tell her what happened.

"So if the cottage is that difficult to access and you've already decided to purchase the lot, then we'll make some sort of arrangement with a larger moving truck and crew. There's no need to bother Mr. Kensey again. Next time I'll simply accompany you and we'll let the hired men do the moving."

"We'll just have to see," I say. Then as nicely as I can I add, "But don't worry, you don't have to be bothered with it. I can take Foster again. I think he actually enjoyed himself today. Thanks for offering though."

She swallows carefully. "So Violet, what do the things look —"

The phone rings and I rush to answer it.

I hope it's Cecil with our new plan.

It's my father.

I explain all about the Vaughn cottage and when I'm done — since it all seems to come out in one breath — he sounds happy and confidently tells me not to worry. He's sure they'll call me back.

But there's something else.

"We talked to someone about Bliss," he says.

"Really?" I lower my voice and turn around. "Someone saw him?"

"Yes. A waitress at a roadside restaurant. She looked at the picture your mother has and was positive."

12

We didn't realize until a few days after Bliss's graduation that he had left. Mom, Dad and I went to the ceremony and sat in the packed, hot, stuffy high school gym along with the entire population of Riverbend. Not a lot of big-deal events happen around here, so the ceremony was something everyone went to whether they were related to a graduate or not. We were in the second row. Dad was in a suit and Mom and I were both wearing dresses. Mom wore her gorgeous antique gold cameo necklace and matching ring Dad had given her for their twentieth wedding anniversary, and everyone was complimenting her on them. She also had a carefully chosen lace hanky in her hand, ready for tears when Bliss got his diploma.

Giant bouquets of pink, purple and white lupines sat on tall pedestal plant stands in each corner of the stage. The seventy-four graduates were in the middle, on two sets of risers, each slightly angled to form a *V*. Bliss and Dean were in the front since they were honour students. Everyone was wearing a long burgundy gown with mustard yellow trim at the neck. Their graduation caps were perched precariously, tassels swinging slightly in the breeze from the three fans set in the front.

The guest speaker that night was an RHS grad from six or seven years ago whose real name was Beryl Brown but who went by Rosalie Sweet. She was a big hometown success story as a country and gospel singer who'd been to Nashville once. Although she currently spent most of her weekends singing at Merle King's Bar in Woodstock. In her speech to the grads, she also went with the old standby but horrible spiel (much the same as the Kings Landing wedding toasts) about them *finally* really starting their lives. I tuned her out as soon as she started quoting lyrics from one of her three original songs as motivational advice. Something about don't hook your dreams to a balloon and let them float away, tie that string down for another day.

I'm sure all the grads were ignoring her too, waiting for her to finish so they could get their diplomas, toss their caps in the air, shake hands down the receiving line, thank and hug teachers whether they wanted to or not, tolerate tears from parents and pose for endless pictures. Afterwards they'd go out to eat with their families at the Irving Restaurant, Davey's Diner or downriver to The Moonlight Motel, then finally go home, change, take their case of beer, pint of rum or bottle of Baby Duck out of hiding and head to the all-night party.

It's a tradition: the big grad party at Haventon Field. The land is just outside Riverbend limits, on an old farmer's acreage that is the only surviving bit of the town of Haventon. It's a beautiful meadow with a gentle slope down to the shore of the river.

On the afternoon of the graduation (the actual ceremony started at six) a bunch of grade elevens helped convert the field into a party zone. Once the field was cut, we raked it. We dug three fire pits. Someone pulled in with a trailer hauling a dozen long logs to be used as seating. And most important of all, two porta-potties showed up on a truck, rented from a place in Fredericton. They would be disgusting within about an hour of the party starting, and eventually everyone would just run down to the treeline or water's edge, but they were there. A miniature city of tents began appearing on the field as grads stopped by to set them up ahead of time. Barkley brought his giant circus-sized contraption for him, Bliss, Dean and Johnny to stay in. There were rows and groups of lawn chairs. People brought Frisbees, footballs, even badminton rackets and birdies.

Jill and I went to the party, nice and early, at nine. Even though the field was outside Riverbend, it was still walking distance to both our houses — about twenty-five minutes — but that night I was sleeping over at Jill's. We stayed at the party a couple of hours, drank only two beers each because Jill's mother was uptight and would be awake and smelling our breath and maybe even getting us to recite the alphabet backwards when we got to her place. It was also an unwritten rule that while the whole school was certainly invited to hang out with the grads, it was their party and for the better part of the night you left them to it.

It was a warm night and there was a half moon, a few clouds in the sky, but plenty of stars. Light coming from the fire pits and the dozens of camping lanterns set here and there gave the field a soft glow. Bliss and Dean and Johnny were playing Frisbee when we went to say goodbye. Jill gave Johnny a hug and a long kiss. I hugged Dean and congratulated him. Then I stepped towards Bliss.

"You too, big brother. You did it," I said.

I hugged him and he hugged me.

"Roger, Roy Rogers," Bliss said.

"Good one," I said.

I studied his face and he smiled. So did I.

Jill took my hand, ready to lead me away.

"So we'll see you guys later," she said.

"Gotta go," I said.

Bliss nodded. "Gotta go."

Then Jill and I ran as if we had to make a quick getaway. We were
laughing and when Jill tripped and almost pulled us both down, I
turned back to see if anyone had noticed. Bliss was standing still,
watching me.

It was almost three in the afternoon before I arrived home from Jill's
the next day. It was a Friday and both my parents were at the store.
The mattress on Jill's top bunk (which she's had since she was six)
wasn't exactly comfortable, so I had slept horribly. I dreamt that all the
Barbies we had played with as kids were mad we were ignoring them
now and they kept head-butting my back. I took a nap as soon as I got
in the house. I woke when Mom phoned a little before five to say that a
tour bus had shown up and to go ahead and eat supper myself. She was
sure that she and Dad would be at least another hour. She asked if Bliss
was back yet but didn't seem concerned in the slightest that he wasn't.
I asked if she wanted me to phone over to Dean's to tell him to come
home, but she said not to bother. Last night had been grad after all.

It was eight o'clock before my parents got home — due to their policy to
never kick a customer out of the store. It was one of those days when
people kept coming. I called over to Dean's then. His mother said he
had decided to sleep back at the field again. A whole bunch of kids
were staying. Bliss too, she figured.

I let my parents know and Dad remembered Bliss mentioning he
would probably stay another night. Staying an extra night was certainly
a common tradition and nothing out of the ordinary.

. . .

But I should have checked. I should have walked there, a nice stroll along the river's edge. It would have been so easy to do. Sure I was tired and lazy and wanted to stay on the couch and watch TV, but I should have gone. I could have even hopped in the truck and taken the five-minute drive. I did manage to get off the couch eventually and go out to the patio, but the cool air hit me. So I went back in and decided to warm up for a second under the afghan. Then I was too warm and cozy and I fell asleep.

I slept until ten the next morning and when I woke my parents were already gone to the store. There was a note on the counter: "If Bliss isn't back by afternoon, track him down."

I called over to Dean's about eleven, figuring they should be awake and back — to see if they wanted to go to The Snack Shack at Seven Birches for fries then stop at the store. Dean wasn't there, and his mother said he and Barkley had gone fishing somewhere way upriver. I asked if Bliss was with them, but she said she didn't think so. I called Barkley's place. Same answer. His mother didn't think Bliss was around.

I walked over to the field and all the tents were gone. I walked to Jill's. She phoned Johnny. He phoned a few people. We phoned a few people. No one had seen Bliss. No one could even remember seeing him the day before. And of course Barkley and Dean, the two people most apt to have a clue, were out of reach.

I think I already knew.

I went home and directly to Bliss's room. As soon as I thought to look for a note I found it. Bliss's graduation cap was sitting on his bed. A folded white square was underneath.

It said:

See ya, Vi.
Gone exploring.
  Love, Bliss.

I dropped down on his bed and stayed very still. It kept me from running out to our deck and screaming after Bliss, even though he could already have been hundreds of miles away.

He was gone. And the note was written to me, not Mom or Dad, as if he knew I would be the one to see it first. I was the one he was telling. I was the first one he was leaving behind.

I phoned my parents to come home. They left Quinny in charge of the store. My mother cried when I showed her the note. She took it from me and sat on a chair at the kitchen table. And although she could read the whole thing, clearly see every bit of information provided, seven words, she kept asking questions as if the answers would appear, as if there was something more written there in invisible ink that she could coax magically to life on the page.

"Well, when did he leave? Where did he go? Did he say when he's coming back? Is he alone? Is he hitchhiking? What did he take with him? How long is he gone for? And exploring? What does that mean — exploring? And why is the note written to you, Violet?"

Her face changed. A realization.

"Violet, did you know he was going? Did he tell you? Why didn't you say anything? Why did you let him go?" There was a terrible urgency in her voice. "Why didn't you stop him?"

She grabbed my arm. She was crying. "Oh, Violet!"

"I didn't know. I didn't."

Mom leaned ahead in the chair to hug me.

My father shook his head and touched my arm. "It's okay, Violet, she's just upset. We all are. You didn't do anything wrong. It was Bliss, not you."

I didn't know. He didn't tell me. No whistle warning this time. Bliss didn't give me a chance to try and make him stay.

I find Quinny in the craft section and tell her that I have to go back out for a minute. I walk directly to my lawn chair by the stream. It's cool in the woods. Calm in the woods. Maybe Foster is onto something.

As far as the Vaughn estate goes, I suppose I can cross my fingers — and toes.

And my parents had news about Bliss. Information to move ahead with. That's what I should concentrate on. But it's hard to keep my mind from wandering. Especially being here in the forest. I try to sit quietly. Breathe.

"Hey Speckles!" I call. "Speckles! You out there? Speccccckles!"

I listen and wait.

"Speckles!"

No response.

"Come here, boy! Speckles!"

Still nothing. Figures. Probably only comes out at night.

I slip off my sandals, move from my chair and sit on a rock at the very edge of the stream. I dunk my feet in the cool water, rest them on submerged green moss. It feels good to squish my toes, knead them, against the spongy surface. A bit of dirt stirs and I can see moss pieces begin to lift and float. I use my toenails to dig and loosen the green edges. More fragments of moss detach and move downstream. Soon enough I feel something more solid. It's small and flat — metal I think. I reach down beneath my big toe and lift out an old brown penny that had been hidden under the moss. It must be one that Bliss and I threw in years ago. We used to have so much fun back here. We'd spend hours and hours. Playing, talking, laughing. I turn the coin over and over in my hand. Then I flick it high in the air, let it flip and spin before it splashes in the water.

I make a wish. But I'm not saying what for. Even though I know it's impossible to spoil a wish for something that can't come true anyway.

13

When Bliss and I were younger, on the Sundays we didn't go to Kings Landing we drove the back roads with Dad as he looked for deserted houses. When he found one, we waited with Mom in the car while he went in and explored. Sometimes he came back empty-handed, but other times he'd return with a treasure. It might be an old piece of fancy moulding pried off a mantel, or a pair of long-forgotten pewter salt and pepper shakers, or once a cast iron doorstop shaped like a little dog.

The idea of an abandoned house creeped me out when I was a kid. It was a hard concept to grasp. Who walks away from a house? Did the whole family die? Why wasn't it sold? Was something wrong with it? Did the people get scared away? Abducted by aliens? And on and on. Sometimes my imagination got away from me, and I'd worry that our house would suddenly turn derelict. I'd worry it would be like a curse dropped over the whole place and it would be instantly transformed. (Like most kids, I had no concept of long periods of time, and I believed devastating life events could only happen all of a sudden.)

If we'd spent the day visiting our grandmother in Fredericton Junction, I'd get edgy two-thirds of the way home. I'd feel as if I had to pee and my hands would turn cold and blotchy. I'd lean ahead so my forehead would rest on the back of Mom's seat. She'd sometimes say, "Tired, Dolly? We're almost home." Which didn't help because

I was envisioning our house as if in a black-and-white photo, our shutters tilting, windows shattered, back deck drooping, driveway poked through with weeds and the garage collapsed. My relief as we rounded the final corner and I saw the house still intact was always incredible.

Really this was a phase that lasted only half a year, five or six instances of such torturous trips home, but it's the kind of thing you don't forget. Dad knew where every abandoned house was in all of York County, so that meant I did too. It seemed they were everywhere. There were certainly enough to make a whole ghost town if they were ever all moved to one location.

As the years went by, my fear turned to curiosity. We could hear the excitement in Dad's voice every time he described what he'd seen or showed us what he'd found. We wanted our chance to explore. So by the time we were ten and eleven, Bliss and I were finally allowed to get out of the car. Except it wasn't at a house, it was at a deserted church.

Mom said we could go as far as the missing front door and look in. I was disappointed. It was grey and dusty and almost empty. Three pews were still inside. They were long low benches made of thick planks with a cloverleaf shape on the end. Some leaves had blown in on the floor. One of the windows was broken and glass shards were strewn beneath it. When a mouse scurried across the floor, I screamed from the surprise of it and ran. Bliss and Dad laughed and stayed put.

Mom was waiting in the car. After she realized I hadn't been attacked by a rabid chipmunk or had a loose board fall on my head, she said it was fine if I looked around the churchyard. It was full of alders, wild raspberry and blackberry bushes, and pink wild roses grown up to within a foot of the building. I was wearing shorts and I knew my legs would get scratched, but I didn't care. I was annoyed about Dad and Bliss laughing, so I decided to scare them by banging on a window. But when I got about halfway down the side of the church I noticed something that changed my mind. There was a small break in the bushes and a single headstone. It was a thick pale grey slab. I went closer and bent branches out of the way until I could see the whole front of it.

There was an angel carved at the top of the headstone. She had long hair and her wings were outstretched. What looked like details of feathers and delicate drape lines in her robe were almost worn away, but her entire outline was visible. Below it said only "Small — In Memory of our Children." No date. I ran my fingers over the angel's wings and got an idea.

I grabbed the crayons and papers that Bliss used for his licence plates from the car. I chose a black crayon to make the rubbing. I put the angel up in my room when we got home. Mom wasn't sure about it. But Dad saw no harm; he said it showed that I appreciated things from the past, the same as he did. It stayed on the wall above my dresser.

Until it got vacuumed the morning we came back from the Woodstock hospital after the Rusty Nail Incident.

Mom had stepped on a rusty nail as a kid. It was sticking out from a fence picket that had fallen to the ground. On a dare from her older sister she ran and hurdled the fence, then came straight down on the unseen nail. She said her vision turned red from pain. My grandmother was beyond furious at them both for being so foolish, but after she calmed down, she tied a piece of salt pork to the bottom of my mother's foot and made her squeeze two socks on over top. That was the cure. My mother said it was agony, torture, like the nail was still in her foot, growing barbs and needles and thorns in every direction up the whole length of it. She had horrible nightmares when she finally fell asleep. She dreamt that every forest animal and sharp-beaked bird was lined up, waiting to take a turn nibbling on the pork, but instead they kept gnawing away at her foot. She remembers it as the worst event of her childhood.

About a month after the visit to the deserted church, Mom finally agreed to let Bliss and me go in an abandoned house. Bliss went in first, and within two seconds he stepped on a piece of the old door frame that had fallen down. Complete with rusty nail. The nail went right through his sneaker and the board attached to his foot like a ski. He wailed in pain.

Dad was still out in the yard of the house and Mom was in the car. Bliss grunted and lifted his foot, but the board was stuck to it. He shook it once, but it didn't come off. He winced.

"Stand on it, Vi," he said. I shook my head. I was scared; I was sure it would hurt him. "You have to," Bliss said. "Just hold it down steady and I'm going to lift my foot again."

I reached for his hand and carefully stepped on the board. I placed my feet so his foot was in the middle of them.

"Okay," I said.

Bliss squeezed my hand.

Then Dad ran in with Mom right behind him. Before they could say anything, Bliss locked eyes with me, gritted his teeth and lifted his foot. The board came off.

We went to the hospital in Woodstock. Bliss had to get a tetanus shot (in the rear) because he needed one. Mom made me get a precautionary one, which was ridiculous — as if she was ever going to let me within ten miles of any rusty nails again. Then the angel disappeared from my room.

When I asked my mother where it went she claimed she accidentally brushed against it when she was vacuuming and it fell and immediately got sucked into the machine. I asked if she tried to get it out, like the time we had to dump a whole bag of dirt outside and dig for one of her earrings, but she said it shredded, she could hear it tearing to bits as it was suctioned. She apologized, "Sorry, Violet, sorry." But I didn't believe her.

Now I know she got rid of the angel because of what she associated it with. She knew where the angel had come from, the chain of events she thought it started. I had overheard Dad telling her it was insane to blame herself, and that stepping on a rusty nail is hardly a near-death experience, it was crazy how much she was making of it. But she wouldn't listen. She saw it only as a reminder of her bad judgment — an unwanted souvenir. Some things told stories. Not all stories had happy endings. For Mom, it was like the angel had a reverse sentimental value. Sad-imental maybe?

Mom thought she should have, or could have, protected Bliss. I get that now. But Bliss's foot got fixed up good as new. It was no big deal, really. His injury and the pain came from a very specific source that could be pinpointed, healed, cured. The Rusty Nail Incident had a very specific beginning, middle and end. I'm not Bliss's mother, but I think I'd take a whole pile of rusty nails, scraped knees, chicken pox, bee stings, twisted ankles, frostbite, sunburn, bloody noses and broken arms over the unseen and seemingly unfixable illness that existed in Bliss. It was something that would appear to go away but then cycle back and make him despair again and again, darken his whole perspective, take away his reasonable judgment and make him forget everything good about himself. It was like an internal enemy that he had to repeatedly fight against and try to break free from.

It was something that would finally make Mom and Dad go searching for him in an attempt to understand.

My mother had no tolerance for my father's declaration that Bliss would come back on his own. Dad said that Bliss was an adult, legally allowed to leave, and he didn't just disappear, he'd left a note. "He's eighteen. He just graduated. I remember being young like that — wanting to get out and see the world." I think he said it in an attempt to calm Mom, but it was the wrong thing to say. Dad made it sound as if what had happened was logical and inevitable. Or as if Bliss had simply mentioned he was planning to go and could still be talked out of it — not already left.

"But it's Bliss," Mom said. Which meant so much.

And the note said so little. Far too little for Mom's liking. It may as well have been a blank page. No clues. No explanation. It almost made things worse Mom said. Because, soon enough, everyone else would miss him as well. And they'd ask questions that it would seem we, as the family, should be able to answer. That was what she said.

But of course, it was really all more than that. She wanted him there. Back. Five minutes ago. Already sitting on the couch. She wanted him there to open the graduation card that had arrived from our old great-aunt Winnie who lived in Saint John. And to compliment her on the pumpkin pie, his favourite, that she'd been planning to take from the freezer for dessert. She wanted him there to tell him that someone finally bought the bizarre antique flycatcher that had been in the store and we figured would never, ever sell. She wanted him there and safe. And the way she stood and stared at his baby picture on our sideboard, I knew she wished, yearned — needed really — in that moment for him to be three years old again so she could tuck him in bed.

Instead she went about trying to fix what she could, talking urgently to my father as I listened at the table. They should call everyone again, and more people, everyone Bliss knew, just to be sure. And they should call the police. Who could they call upriver? (Because if there was one thing they knew for sure it was that he had gone upriver, not down. Towards Quebec or Maine, not the other way, through Nova Scotia, where the land ran out and the dead-end ocean came too soon.)

So Mom got on the phone and asked everyone I'd already asked the same questions. She phoned Barkley's mother and talked to Barkley and Dean. They hadn't seen Bliss since Friday around noon. They said he had stayed up almost all night and claimed he was going home to crash. He wasn't back at the campsite that night. They just figured he was beat and still sleeping, expected he'd probably show up later. Mom stared out the window as she listened, repeated, had them repeat. Her expression changed. She was scared.

Bliss wasn't just gone, but long gone.

I get up from the side of the stream and sit in my lawn chair again. I'll go back to the store soon. Get on with my day. Make some money. Make some tourists happy. Business has been good. I am good at this. But first, for a minute or two, I tilt my head back, slouch sideways in the lawn chair, gaze up through layers of dark spriggy branches, silhouettes upon silhouettes all the way up to the sky.

It's the last thing I remember doing before I fall asleep. And at first my dreams are a loop of me organizing shelf after shelf of plain white vases in the barn, then Pepper Shaker jumping and racing around, knocking everything to the floor with a dramatic crash. But somehow nothing breaks, so I have to start again. Pick up, neaten, reset, cat, fall and crash, over and over. Then everything changes and I'm at the Vaughn cottage, in the rainbow room. Pepper Shaker is still a destructive streak, glass falling everywhere. And this time breaking. Tiny pretty glass pieces are all over the place, which I start to pick up one by one. I hear an angry scream from outside the rainbow room and look up to see a boy with dead eyes, dripping wet, even his skin oozing water. I jump back and promptly cut my hand in a thousand places with a thousand pretty sparkles of colour.

A touch on my arm. I turn and it's Speckles who has nudged me with his nose. Bliss is beside him.

"Need a Band-Aid for that, Vi?" he asks.

I wake up.

Jill is beside me. She's the one who touched my arm. "You okay, Vi?"

"Oh. Hey, yeah?" I look down at my right hand. I've dug my fingernails deep enough into it that there are dark red ripples across my palm.

"What time is it?" I look around.

"Almost four."

I slept most of the afternoon. And it's kind of weird that Jill's here. Still dressed like she stepped out of a time machine too.

"Dean sent you?"

"Maybe. Come on. We're working until five, then the boys have a little supper surprise."

"We're working?"

"Yes. We. Dean left and I'm here instead. And I already got stopped in the parking lot on the way back here and posed for a picture, so obviously I fit right in."

"And do I dare ask about the supper surprise?"

"All I know is Dean and Johnny are coming up with something. Then all four of us are hanging out together at the cottage for the rest of the weekend."

We step beyond the trees and walk across the meadow. As we get closer to the playground and picnic tables, I notice some of the tourists start turning their heads. It's Jill's outfit. The parking lot has about a dozen cars. A woman carrying one of Foster's little twig tables comes out the front door of the barn as we go in. I send Elizabeth and Quinny home early. Jill and I have the whole store to ourselves. Jill stays near the front door and acts as a hostess, welcoming customers. She's friendly and everyone seems happy to see her. Almost every single customer buys at least a postcard for the next hour. The time passes quickly, and when I realize it's already twenty after five, we start bringing in things from the display outside.

"Told you I'd be good for business," Jill says.

"What do I owe you?"

"Not a thing. Just be sure you have some fun tonight," she says. "I'd say this dinner is pretty above and beyond on Dean's part so please, best effort. Here and now. Good times. Okay?"

"Grin and bear it. Can do."

Jill rolls her eyes.

The phone rings.

"I bet that's Dean now wondering when we'll be down." She picks up the phone. "The Purple Barn Antiques. Jill speaking. How may I help you?" She winks at me.

"Oh, just a second, I'm not sure if she's gone yet," Jill says. She puts her hand over the receiver. "Cecil?" she whispers.

I rush towards her. "Cecil, I'm so glad you called," I say.

"Well I thought I might just catch you rather than have to wait 'til Monday. Now I don't have a new time for you—and honestly I hate to say it—but I'm afraid I might not. The lawyer had some big offer for absolutely everything, house contents included. But Mr. Vaughn's got to check with the rest of the family back home, see what they think. I told him you were ready to take it and he appreciated that, but now we'll just have to wait and see."

I feel ill.

"I suppose they just want it all done with the least amount of hassle," I say. I look over in Jill's direction, but she's gone back outside.

"Maybe, but I did put in a good word, so we'll see. I wanted you to know so you weren't wondering, thinking we forgot about you. A couple more days and we should know either way."

"Okay, thanks, Cecil. Thanks." I hang up.

I stay on the chair behind the counter and slide my hands under my thighs.

Jill comes back in carrying a picture frame.

"All done? So grinning and bearing from here on out, right, Vi? You're going to suffer through this special evening, arranged by your fabulous boyfriend, with a smile on your face."

I nod.

"Right, Vi?" Jill asks again. She stops walking and waits until I respond.

"For sure, try my best," I say. "Really, watch, starting right now." I take a deep breath, smile and hop off the chair.

We both head back out to get the rest of the things from the display.

"It was Cecil Haines who called, right?" Jill says. "Was it something about the Vaughn estate?" Jill asks.

"Yeah," I say. "But it really wasn't anything exciting. He was just double-checking something."

"So who is it that's down here anyway?" Jill asks. "Johnny's mom actually remembered a lot about the Vaughns and said that Ivy had two sons — who both would be in their late fifties now, she figured. So is your Mr. Vaughn one of them?"

"It must be," I say. "I've never talked to him. The first couple of phone calls to set it up Quinny answered and it was a woman anyway — his wife I guess."

Jill helps me lift a trunk.

"I wonder if it's the parents of the boy who drowned?"

"I don't know."

"He was trying to rescue someone when it happened. Swam out to get him or something."

"I hadn't heard that."

We set the trunk down.

"An old lady Johnny's mom knew growing up went to Ivy's legendary tea party, you know. She said the Vaughns had sterling silver for their everyday forks and spoons, and so many chairs and rockers that you'd never have to go more than six feet without sitting down."

"Well, I don't know that there are that many," I say.

"When you do get the estate I'm going to try to convince Johnny to let me come buy some of the things for our place."

"*Our* place?"

"You know what I mean. We're going to need a lot. I can't wait to start getting everything. Gram's got some stuff set aside for us too that she said we could have now — whenever the time comes."

I put the last item from outside — an old milk can — into the store, then I lock the door.

"Marked with your name?" I ask.

"Oh yes, carefully marked."

She laughs and we head for the truck.

Jill's grandmother had a heart attack early, a scare at fifty-nine, and as soon as she was home from the hospital, she went through her house with a roll of masking tape and a pen, putting labels on things. Now every vase, plant stand, TV tray and figurine has a name on the bottom. Jill helped her do it. They organized her entire accumulation of future heirlooms.

Once I went with Jill to visit her grandmother, and sure enough, as she tipped up her teacup for a final sip, I could see a masking tape square on the bottom. Jill says the family teases her sometimes at Thanksgiving and Christmas dinners, lifting their plates, looking for names, like they're seeing if there's an *X* and they've won the door prize. Her grandmother gets a good giggle out of it though, Jill says — and knowing it's all taken care of helps her sleep at night.

. . .

The campground is full. I can smell barbeques, a waft of propane from a Coleman stove, woodsmoke and the faint scent of fly dope coming off a kid who runs by us. Jill and I walk the long circular roadway that passes most of the sites. Towels and bathing suits hang drying from tree branches. Jill picks up an empty chip bag and puts it in one of the green metal garbage barrels. A blue ball bounces onto the road in front of us and a little boy races to grab it. He darts behind a pop-top trailer with orange and beige canvas sides. It has an Ontario licence plate and there are others from Quebec, Vermont and PEI. The Prince Edward Island one is black and yellow with the slogan "Seat Belts Save." As we walk on, we see that Nova Scotia is "Canada's Ocean Playground." Maine is "Vacationland." Alberta is "Wild Rose Country."

Dean and Johnny are still preparing supper. And by *preparing* I mean heating up several casseroles in the oven and unpacking a massive box of food. They drove over to Riverbend and both their mothers contributed. From their families' freezers they have four casseroles, a tin of shortbread cookies and two pies. Johnny's mother also sent a dozen rolls, a plate of fresh-cut cucumbers and tomatoes from her garden and a potato salad. Dean's mother sent biscuits, half a ham roast sliced up and a jar of her Lady Ashburnham pickles. It's too much, of course, but so sweet of them to do. It's like a church potluck squeezed into our tiny kitchen. Jill and I were told to scram for half an hour. The banquet will be ready upon our return.

It smells good when Jill and I get back to the cottage.

"So here are our women now," Johnny says.

He's in the kitchen with Dean — and our next-door neighbour is with them. Jill looks at me and raises her eyebrows.

"We invited one more," Dean says. "Since we've got enough food to feed an army. Of course Johnny here rushed him once he showed up in that car."

"Pretty groovy ride," Johnny adds.

"I'm Ivan," our neighbour says. "Ivan Longwood."

Jill and I introduce ourselves and we sit down to eat. Ivan tells us that he's twenty-one and just graduated from university in Montreal. He's been doing some landscaping work he picked up nearer to Fredericton. He's in New Brunswick for the summer, seeing the sights before he looks for a real job in the fall. He says that he's down here "exploring," and the word gives me a sudden pang. It makes me think of Bliss. I take a drink of water. Maybe that's why I couldn't help but wonder about Ivan staying at the campsite, if I unknowingly sensed something vaguely familiar in him. Ivan's telling us his parents wanted him to take the summer off, come down here, look around, take it all in. It was their idea, but he claims he didn't need to be convinced. Ivan was keen to see new scenery, have new experiences. Which is so much what Bliss wanted, what he hoped for.

Ivan gestures his arms widely and smiles. "Meet new people," he says.

I turn to look out the window. I wonder who Bliss met along the way. I wonder what he'd say to them.

"You sell some at the store, don't you, Vi?"

"Vi. Vi?" Jill says.

"Oh sorry, what?"

"Ivan here was complimenting the Lady Ashburnham pickles Dean's mom sent, and I told him it was a local specialty," Jill says. "But you sell some for the tourists don't you?"

"You're right, we do. And chokecherry jelly if you need any of that."

"You work in a grocery store?" Ivan asks.

"Vi's an antique dealer," Dean says and smiles at me.

"My dad owns The Purple Barn," I say. I point at an angle towards the back wall of the cottage. "It's kind of up there. I'm sure you've seen it — it's pretty hard to miss. But my parents are away so I'm in charge."

Ivan looks a little confused, as if I really haven't answered his question.

"Well, Violet, I can't say I'd ever have guessed," he says.

"She's a pro too," Dean says. "Total expert. Don't let that pretty face fool you."

"I don't know about a pro," I say.

"You are," Jill says. "I've heard you talking to customers."

"So will you take over the business someday?" Ivan asks.

"Maybe."

"Well I think that's very cool. I'm glad to meet you."

We eat and eat. Ivan seems sincerely interested in the whole antiques business and talks to me more about it. I suppose I could end up running The Purple Barn — way in the future. Even though it's officially called Charles J. Davis and Son Antiques, Dad never assumed that Bliss would take it over when he was older. There was no pressure or obligation there. Dad claims that he simply thought adding "And Son" to the name made it traditional sounding, and if any business should have an old-fashioned name, it is one that deals in antiques. Who knows what would have happened — with anything really — if I had been born first. Bliss used to talk about maybe being a veterinarian. I still haven't decided for myself, beyond going to university in Fredericton. And there are other things to figure out first.

After supper we all play Frisbee then head down to the beach for a while. Ivan tells us stories about living in Montreal. We swim and splash and take turns jumping off the dock. Then we all have a few beers and sing along with Dwayne at the campfire before Ivan has to go.

The next day is Sunday so we spend the whole day at Seven Birches. Ivan waves at Dean from the pay phone in the morning, but then he is gone, "exploring" for the day I guess. The four of us have lunch at The Snack Shack. We play in Dwayne's annual summer horseshoe tournament. Jill and I finish fourth. Dean and Johnny finish fifth. We go back to the beach. We have leftovers for supper and still don't finish all the food. We sit on the porch and watch the sun setting.

Eventually I take Dean to bed with me. It starts to rain. I hear the drops on the roof. I listen to their rhythm, and Dean's heartbeat, my head on his chest. I think only: I am here. I am now. This is good. I am good.

14

If it was a slow day at the store, Bliss and I were allowed to play hide-and-seek. There were always lots of places to hide, and as the furniture and other stock in the store changed, the best spots to hide changed. Old favourites were big cupboards to squeeze behind, a bed to go under or a giant barrel to get in. But sometimes there was a cedar chest or a tall hall stand with a mirror and hooks, or a giant copper steamer or a stack of two dozen wooden pop crates to keep us well concealed.

Once I even managed to hide in plain sight by quickly pulling my hair back in a ponytail, grabbing my sun visor, throwing on Mom's coat and posing as a customer. There was a lady by herself in the store and I hovered near her, looking at everything she looked at as if I was her daughter. Mom was in on it and even came over to us like she was asking if we needed anything. I kept my back to Bliss whenever I heard him coming. He must have looked for twenty minutes before he finally gave up and Mom brought him over to me. He didn't look too pleased to have been stumped. Mom laughed and so did I.

A few days later Bliss suggested he and I hide from Mom and Dad just before closing. (I think it was his idea of retaliation.) Bliss chose a tall, mahogany-stained wardrobe for our spot. After Mom gave us the ten-minute warning that we'd be going home, we disappeared behind its doors. Inside the wardrobe was dark and stale smelling, and after five minutes I was ready to get out. But when I reached to push the door open Bliss grabbed my arm. So I waited, thinking it was no big deal to stay a few more minutes. Mom and Dad started calling for us. Of course I figured they'd conclude we were playing a game, joking around, and that they'd enjoy the search, bending down to look under beds, peek behind things, open furniture doors, lift lids of trunks and big tea boxes. Then I heard Mom tell Dad she was checking outside, which I knew meant the parking lot and the highway. Her voice already sounded anxious.

I started to call Mom but Bliss covered my mouth. I swatted and pushed at him as we heard Mom go out the door. Then he put both arms around me to try to keep me from getting out. The movement toppled the whole wardrobe. Which was scary enough and it hurt when we hit the floor, but the domino effect it started was worse. I heard another bang and shattering glass — lots and lots of shattering glass — and another heavy thud with cracks and crunches followed by softer thuds. Then the rush of air of something tall tilting, falling, scraping a surface on the way down. Dad, who I guess was still in the store, came running. Mom rushed back in from outside.

They were so mad at us. Mom likes to say that people don't get mad; only animals go mad, people get angry. But not this time.

"Jesus Christly H. Christ," Dad yelled. "What the —" and he shook his head.

Once we were free, I could see that the shattering glass was not only the doors on an antique walnut china cabinet, but also the entire antique glass and china contents. The big thud was a bookcase. The little thuds were the books. The books hadn't been hurt of course, but the case itself landed on a small table with a display of antique sweetgrass baskets. The baskets were destroyed. The thing that had tilted and fallen was an oak coat rack. One of the hooks had scraped a beautiful painting on the way down. There was a crooked line like a lightning strike through the pastoral scene. A tall cranberry glass lamp had also broken in at least a hundred pieces.

I proclaimed it was all Bliss's fault, but it didn't matter. So he was mad at me along with Mom and Dad, and I was mad at him. For punishment we had to spend the next Saturday entirely in the storage room. We were allowed out only to use the washroom. The damage added up to more than a thousand dollars. (Dad had to count it to take the amount out of his books.) But it wasn't the money that upset my parents the most.

I heard Mom telling Dad after that she thought we were gone, and the fact that we gave her that horrible feeling was the worst part of what we'd done. There were times when her mind jumped to a disastrous conclusion way too quickly. Sure parents are allowed to worry, but she seemed to have an extra share of fear and anxiety. I think it came from the uncertainty she felt about Bliss.

When I open the door of the barn to start the day, Quinny's husband George is coming out.

"Another quilt delivery?" I ask.

"No, not today," he says. "Just dropping Alvina in so I can keep the car and run some errands. You're looking as lovely as always." He smiles at me.

He seems like such a nice man. And Jill said he was a good math teacher. A little excitable about the thrills of geometry maybe, but he always tried hard to explain things and never made his students feel stupid.

"Thanks." I remove a long piece of thread that I notice clinging to George's shirt. He looks down and quickly takes another off one of his pant legs.

"Worse than cat hair," he says and shakes his head. He laughs but seems embarrassed.

Our first customer of the day pulls into the lot and parks pretty much right at our feet.

"Well, have a good day, Violet," George says.

"Thanks, I'll try."

I go inside. I fill Pepper Shaker's water bowl and feed him. Then I take my position behind the counter. It's Monday morning, start of a fresh new week. This is my job. This is my family's business. This is where my parents want me to be this summer.

The front door opens and it's Mrs. Harris of spaghetti-poodle fame stopping in again, even though she was here just the other day. She's wearing a dress that looks like a deflated hot air balloon in a pattern of giant poppies on a turquoise background.

"Violet, hello dear," she says. "Goodness, you're here early, and even behind the counter. I quite expected Alvina."

"She's here too," I say. "If—"

"Well, no, no. I'll ask you, Violet. Any new wee doggies?"

She really has on a lot of poinsettia-coloured sparkly lipstick. I wonder how many times both clockwise and counter-clockwise she circles around her lips with the tube.

"You know, we might," I say. "I think Dad actually had one saved for you. I'll go see."

She clasps her hands together.

I head to The Room. I'm positive there's one in there. Last year Dad found a group of fifteen spaghetti poodles at a yard sale. The five that are left are lined on a shelf. One at a time he doles them out to her, as if he is constantly on the lookout on her behalf. Quinny doesn't know about them, so it's only when she asks Dad (or now me) that she has luck. We don't put them out on the display floor as a courtesy, so no one buys one out from under Mrs. Harris before she gets a chance to come over. I choose a little grey dog this time with black cat eye glasses — a rare find. Almost all the spaghetti poodles we get are pink or white and certainly aren't in spectacles.

Out at the counter Quinny and Mrs. Harris are chatting away. When I unveil the new porcelain pet, Mrs. Harris laughs with delight.

Quinny says, "Well, isn't that a lovely one, now." But then rather than staying to talk longer or take over the cash register from me, Quinny leaves and goes to ask a lady in the craft section if she needs any help.

Mrs. Harris buys the poodle — five dollars, same price as always — and I wrap it in several pieces of newspaper so it survives the trip home. She's quiet, watching, glancing alternately down to see that I am doing a good job and back up at me and smiling.

"So, Violet," she finally says, "you went to see the Vaughn cottage I heard."

Of course.

"Yes, no poodles there, though."

"But you bought the things? Are they as nice as everyone figures? You know, I remember years ago hearing that Ivy had the most beautiful oval hall mirror with a frame all carved with roses."

I nod. "So are you enjoying your summer off from teaching?" I ask.

"Oh," she says. "Yes, I suppose. I do love my students but a vacation is always nice. And how about your parents' vacation, Violet? Have you heard from them? Are they enjoying themselves?"

"They are," I say. "Thanks for asking." I put the wrapped poodle in a bag and pass it to her. "Here y—"

Mrs. Harris speaks at the same time. "Where was it they went again?" she asks.

"Oh, lots of places — kind of like a road trip."

"And they'll be back soon?"

"Pretty soon, I think," I say. "Pretty soon."

When Mom woke up after the first full night that she knew for sure Bliss was gone, she had devised a plan to do her best to deal with what had happened. She had no choice but to desperately latch on to Dad's belief that Bliss would be back on his own. She could accept the idea herself, so the next step was to convince everyone else of it as well. That was of course a part of small-town living. She knew how it would look: her son went without giving her a chance to stop him. An escape. She couldn't let it appear as though she was the type of mother whose child would skip out of town without a kiss goodbye, because that would make her feel even worse. There would be the inevitable gossip and whispers anyway, speculation on the *real* reasons for Bliss's departure. But since it was summer, and he had just graduated, his trip could be easily enough explained as an adventure. "Gone exploring" — he had said it himself. We had to accept it; it was true. We'd simply wait for the first phone call or postcard. There was little else to do — by the time we clued in, he likely had at least a two-day head start. Quebec, Ontario, Maine, New Hampshire, Vermont — even Boston was only an eight-hour drive away. He could be anywhere.

We had a family meeting. My mother woke me early, before my parents left for the store. She told me to come down to the dining room where Dad sat waiting. There was a piece of paper on the table. It was a new note, written by my mother, with all the missing information she wished Bliss had provided. This new note was to be the new reality outside the house. It gave enough information to stop questions. It was enough information that Mom could adjust her presentation of what had happened not with anxiety or worry, but more with the attitude of an exasperated boys-will-be-boys.

It was in point form to help us remember:

- *Went alone as a celebration of his recent graduation — a special adventure.*
- *Didn't mention to anyone beforehand so he could go alone rather than feeling bad saying no to friends who may wish to join him.*
- *Will call and report in with postcards now and then.*
- *Will certainly be back by summer's end. Likely sooner.*
- *Took lots of money he had saved so he will be able to eat well and stay in nice campsites or hotels.*

My mother had obviously thought a lot about this. She was making the best of the situation, pretending, wishing, maybe even *willing*, this is how it really was. I could feel her watching me closely as I read every point. She twisted a piece of her hair with her finger.

"Okay, Violet?" she finally asked. "We can't have everyone thinking that Bliss just took off like he couldn't wait to get away from us. That he was ungrateful for his good life and future here. That's not him. We know that's not really him. And you know because we're always at the store it means anyone, anytime, can come talk to us, ask us anything. We can't keep to ourselves on this."

My mother looked at me. Tears were starting, turning her eyes glassy. Dad stood and put his arm around her, kissed her forehead. I wondered what Dad really thought — how much of what he said and did was a brave front and how much was a true belief that Bliss could return any second.

"It's fine," I said. "Except not the last one — eat well and stay in hotels? I know you hope he does, but it's a bit much. No one is going to ask or care about that."

"Okay," she nodded.

I pushed my chair back.

"Violet," she said. "Wait." She looked at my father and then back at me. "I, we, need you to say that you actually knew, that Bliss had confided in you, but made you promise not to tell anyone until after."

At first I didn't say anything. It seemed very quiet in the house. I looked at the door and desperately tried to send an ESP message to Bliss, to try to make him walk through it.

"Violet?"

"Why?" I asked.

"Because that really makes the most sense. Violet, we're a family. A good family. I think any parent would understand that maybe your child doesn't tell you everything — of course they don't — but this, nothing? Nothing? He is such a good son. I can understand him not telling me, knowing I'd say no, try to stop him, be worried sick. But as a good son, don't you think he'd be sure I really was okay with it after. Don't you think he would have left a message with you: Tell Mom not to worry. Tell Mom I'll be back soon. Don't you think so, Violet? I mean, you two were so close, not much more than a year apart, almost my little twins. So didn't he? Even hint?" Her voice was becoming more urgent. "Or leave me a message with you? Didn't he? He should have. He must have. Brother and sister. So it's what we have to say. It would really make the most sense." Then the tears slipped out the edges of her eyes.

She needed this. I could see that. An unhappy child was a parent's worst failure. She was already so sad, she didn't need the judgment of others making it worse. And I knew it wasn't just about *appearances* to others, but how it appeared to her. If I agreed, it would calm her. It's not like Bliss was going to call me out for lying once he got back. I figured it was probably no big deal to go along with. It was a way I could help Mom feel better, beyond that I didn't think.

"Okay."

She let out a little gasp, then sighed.

"And you can never waiver, Violet. You have to say you actually knew, and you can't tell Jill or Dean or anyone any different. We're a family. And family comes first."

So to this day that's what everyone believes. That I knew all along and that I didn't try to stop him. That I was the only one with a chance to make it right and I didn't. I've had to commit to the thought so fully that often I find myself wondering if it could be true. I was the one who let everyone down. I knew — should have known — he was going to leave. I didn't stop him. I just let him go.

It's not long until Quinny joins me at the counter. The store is busy enough that people are coming steadily to the cash. Quinny is writing out receipts and taking money and I'm wrapping and bagging their purchases. There are tourists, but there are also a few fine citizens of Riverbend. Maybe it's a coincidence, and they were planning to stop by today anyway, but we've heard more than once, "Oh, and by the way, are the things from the Vaughn estate here?" I did not and will not mention that Cecil phoned and now the situation is more iffy than ever.

To make matters worse, Lolly Perkins, another regular customer, comes in right before noon. Lolly doesn't collect anything specific but buys what *speaks* to her. She's someone who can turn something like an ordinary old second-hand wooden rolling pin into an object of myth. "Oh, if these things could talk," she always says. Everything comes with possible backgrounds and made-up stories of whose hands worked the rolling pin to bake a pie for the church picnic, which led to whose courtship and marriage. She says she likes to feel things that have been used by another person's hands. She likes to have that *connection*.

I try to dodge her when I see her. The stuff in our store isn't wondrous or magic. A spoon is most likely just an old spoon. Not every old object in the whole universe is responsible for triggering a plot twist in someone's life story. The way Lolly Perkins goes on, it's as if she's trying to conjure up ghosts to follow her home. I imagine she dreams of living in a house full of gracious spirits that are enchanted by her interest in their pasts. Maybe sometime she will wake in the night to an angry screeching ghost at the end of her bed, demanding its stuff back.

I see Lolly as she comes in the front door because I'm still at the counter. Her entry is definitely my cue to leave for the bathroom before she discovers some old silver baby cup with a dent that obviously belonged to a feisty little thing with a good arm. She heads right for us though, far too quickly for me to flee.

"Alvina," she says. She knows Quinny from church, and I'm sure she would have heard about the Vaughn estate after yesterday's service, so this must be a regular shopping trip. "And Violet," she adds, glancing to me for a second. But then she leans in to Quinny.

"So what brings you by today, Lolly?" Quinny asks.

"They might have left, you know," she says. "The people staying down here that I was mentioning who everyone figures must be Mr. and Mrs. Vaughn. I stopped by to see Luella at the Falls Motel this morning, and she said they were checked out for good, gone back to Ontario. Did you get any more word about the estate? Or have they stopped by here to meet you yet?" She doesn't wait for Quinny to answer. "Oh my soul, I think sending that odd Foster Kensey down may well have been a giant mistake on Charles's part."

She glances in my direction, but I pretend not to be paying attention. I continue unfolding newspapers to use for wrapping. "My land, what was he thinking? He normally seems like such a smart, sensible man. I know ever since —" A pause. And I can sense she's shifted her eyes towards me. "But this? I just don't know. It looks like he may have ruined his chance."

Quinny's face greys slightly as Lolly Perkins talks. Everything Lolly's saying is rumour, all based on questionable clue-gathering and assumptions, straight-out guessing and gossip to fill in the gaps in the story. But I can tell that Quinny has no idea what to say.

If it's true that we don't end up buying the contents of the estate, we're going to need to spin a much better public relations story than Dad sent Foster and creeped them out — right out of town, that is.

Quinny glances at me, obviously thinking. She adjusts her glasses slightly.

"We'll just have to see," she finally says to Lolly. "We certainly don't know anything for sure yet. But now tell me, have you made any of your strawberry-raspberry jam this year? You know if you ever had any extra I'm sure it would be a real treat for the tourists if you sold some here."

"Oh. No, no," she says. "I've made a few bottles up, but just enough for family and Christmas. But my soul, that estate," she says, not fooled by Quinny's attempted redirection. "Such a shame, Alvina, if it doesn't work out. I know lots of us around here would certainly love to see all those beautiful things. I'm sure there'd be at least a treasure or two I'd need to take home with me. But now, heaven knows." Lolly shakes her head then turns and walks to the door.

Quinny follows her, and I can tell she'd like to grab her arm and shush her like a child, tell her to bite her tongue. Quinny is desperate to quell Lolly's urge to spread the story before she has a chance to come up with proper counterpoints to it — true or not.

"Well, we'll just hope for the best," is all she manages. "Certainly nothing's final yet."

Lolly is out the door and Quinny's coming back towards me. I'm sure I'm about to get an earful, but also the look in her eyes makes me fear for the safety of the inventory, as if she's ready to swoop her arm along a whole shelf of glassware in frustration. Pepper Shaker jumps off a wicker chair as she walks past, and he runs for cover under a sideboard.

The phone rings. My arm is a blur, I grab the receiver so quickly.

"Oh, Cecil," I say. A swirl in my stomach. Quinny doesn't even pretend she's not listening. She stares right at me. This isn't going to be good.

"Yes, yes, so hot again," I say, and I wish he'd just get it over with.

I listen longer. A small miracle has occurred.

"Saturday afternoon? No, I don't mind waiting until then at all," I say. And I swear my legs go weak from relief. "I'm so glad you called. It really is such a lovely estate."

At the word estate, when Quinny is finally absolutely certain, she races out the door, I'm sure in hopes Lolly Perkins's car will still be in the parking lot. I imagine her taking a flying leap, grabbing for the back fender.

15

No one questioned anything we said. I repeatedly heard my mother and father tell the story of Bliss leaving. Quinny learned the details too, simply from asking my parents and hearing it all again and again. She would tell the same tale with knowing authority to anyone who asked. People typically responded with smiles and nods and then the assertion that surely he'd be back sooner or later — for some silly reason. You know, like he'd miss my mother's cooking or he'd run out of clean clothes.

I could tell Mom took comfort in it. Or seemed to in public. Any concerns she had seemed to be easily dismissed by the people she spoke to. It reminded me of when my great-aunt, who was a wonderful piano player, died, Quinny declared that God must have needed a new accompanist for the angel choir. Platitudes. False comfort. Every quaint statement by a neighbour or customer made the expanded story that my mother had spun more and more true. I could tell she was convincing herself by the way she laughed and hugged people — relieved — and threw out little comments about this really just proving Bliss's strong will or adventurous spirit, independent nature or stand-up attitude, even a determination to take his life into his own hands. He obviously took after his father, she'd say. And look at what his father's drive in life had brought him. Such success. It made me feel sad and nervous to hear her. Mom was going along with it all.

At home she was completely different. She wasn't calm or cool. The TV couldn't be turned up to more than a whisper. The same with the radio. She didn't vacuum. Or run the blender. She wouldn't use anything that could drown out the sound of the phone, the doorbell, a yell from the yard. She was a nervous wreck if ever all three of us left the house together to drive to the barn. She pleaded with Dad to go faster and faster and once even tried to get him to pass a car on the Pokiok Bridge. Time we spent driving was time that there was no one to answer the phone at either the house or the barn. What if Bliss called? Mom was always out of the car before Dad even had it into park, running for the door with her key already pointed towards the lock.

Foster had a different reaction to the fact that Bliss was gone. Five days after Bliss left, I was in the field picking wildflowers to fill the vases in the store when I heard Foster's voice. He had come from the forest and was standing at the edge of the field.

"So where'd your brother take off to?" he asked.

I think I flinched. How could Foster know?

"What?"

"Bliss, he's not here, is he?"

Foster's makeshift sled piled with his little twig tables was next to him. Sitting beside that were another three tables bundled together with rope, which he must have been carrying over his shoulder. Bliss hadn't gone out to help him as usual. That was what he meant. Foster seemed unaware that Bliss wasn't just missing a day's work at the store, but wasn't around at all. I didn't know what or how much to say.

Foster stared at me.

"Oh, yeah. No," I said.

He seemed to wait for more, for me to offer an explanation. I looked away and quickly picked two flowers, yanking them as if I didn't grab them right that second, they'd be sucked back into the earth.

"So he finally went, eh?" Foster said behind me.

At the same time my father came out the back of the barn and called to Foster. He must have seen us out the window. In a matter of seconds, he was at Foster's side picking up the bundle of tables.

"Let me get that," Dad said. "Sorry, but Bliss isn't here. Meant to get out to help you myself, but the store's been real busy, time got away on me."

I stole a look at Foster. He didn't challenge my father, ask him anything different, only thanked him for the help and went inside.

I took the flowers in to Elizabeth, then went back out, to my lawn chair by the stream. There were two chairs then — the other was for Bliss. I would wait for Foster. He said *finally*. As if it was some inevitable occurrence that was a long time coming. As if Foster had been waiting for this to happen.

As if Bliss had said something to him.

Foster seemed to take a long time in the store, and I worried that he'd decided to hitchhike to Riverbend for groceries. Eventually I saw his silhouette coming across the field, the sled behind him empty. I stood and turned my chair around, rested my hands on the back of it, as if it was a shield between us.

Foster spoke before he was even in the treeline.

"I don't know anything, Violet," he said. It didn't seem like he was going to stop walking.

"What did you mean — so he *finally* went then?" He came a bit closer and lifted his sled under his arm, but then began walking again.

He took several more steps, stopped and turned.

"Look, Violet, I overheard that gossipy old bat in there tell the whole story to someone when your father went to get my money. But he himself didn't say a word about it. So that tells me it's your family's business and none of mine."

"But you seem like you know something we don't."

He shook his head. He looked at me briefly then shifted his stare past me, out beyond the meadow, to the large purple rectangle that was the barn.

"I don't know anything different than what I just heard. I'm not surprised, that's all. Okay?"

He began to walk. I followed. So Foster had guessed. But he must have had a reason to. I stepped on the heel of Foster's boot. He had stopped walking and I didn't notice. He took his sled from under his arm and turned around again.

"It's this. And don't get excited thinking it's some big secret, it's not. Bliss is a good kid, but I know he only ever came out to my place because your Dad sent him. And he'd ask me what animals I'd seen, ask if I'd seen Speckles, but he never asked me anything about myself.

"Then a while back, let's say a month or so now, he turns serious one day, even asks if we can go inside my cabin, sit down for a minute. He says he wants to know if I'm happy back by myself in the woods, the first personal thing he's ever asked of me. Did moving from my old house to there make me feel happy? Do I like it now just being in one spot, never going anywhere? But I didn't feel I had to explain myself so I said 'Yeah, I'm good. It's good.' Anyway, I can tell it annoys him, and at first I think it's because I didn't explain better, but then I realize that it's really because he knows it's true. That I'm good.

"That's it. Okay? I really don't want to sound unkind, but you make of it what you want."

At the time, I figured that Foster was confirming Bliss did indeed want a change of scenery. That was nothing new. Even his note had said "Gone exploring." And it wasn't until quite a while after that I started to think what Foster was really saying was that he thought Bliss was frustrated because Foster had found a way to be happy (and happy with so little), and Bliss could not.

Of course everyone is looking for happiness, and Bliss was only eighteen — with years ahead to find it. And sure he was happy sometimes. I could sense it. See it. Bliss could still be the fun carefree guy he was as a little kid. But he knew it wouldn't last. It never seemed to last.

My mother says she named him Bliss because that is what she felt the day he was born. It was her way of transferring her happiness to him, bestowing it on him, letting him carry it around with him his whole life. She did it as a celebration, a reminder to herself, but as time went on I think it sometimes weighed him down like an expectation that had to be lived up to.

Mom would sometimes say that Bliss was *in a funk*. He could be moody. Broody? But not always — right? That was the equalizer. And Bliss was a teenager. An awkward teenager. It's an unpredictable stage of life, ever-changing. Dad often said to give Bliss time, let him work it out. Adults know that people can grow up, grow out of things. It's like simply maturing can be the solution, the cure-all for so many teenage problems. Sure Mom was concerned. But it seemed whatever worry she built up vanished once Bliss seemed (at least temporarily) happy again.

It took me a long time to put it together, but I think that's all that Bliss had gone looking for — a more permanent happiness, if such a thing exists. Bliss wondered if changing things outside would help change things inside him too. That's what he was exploring — that possibility. And I did hope so much, at the time, that he found a way to be happy, to clear his head of every unwanted bad thought, to heal himself. But even if it was selfish of me, I hoped he wouldn't find so much happiness elsewhere that he'd fear wrecking it if he came back.

. . .

After six days with no news Dean came to the house. It was in the afternoon, and both my parents were at the barn. Dean sat beside me on the living-room couch.

"Did you hear anything today?" he finally asked.

I shook my head.

"It's weird, you know," he said. "I mean, weird even for Bliss."

I nodded but Dean was looking down and didn't see me.

"Yeah, I know."

"And not so much the taking off, but going and then just nothing. It's like he's completely disappeared — fell off the edge of the Earth. That's what I don't get. Why'd he bother telling you he was going and then pull this?"

I shrugged. I looked away, out the window to the driveway. I could feel the tears forming in me. Droplets first. Beading. Pooling. Then a stream flowing to my eyes. I couldn't look at Dean. I ran my tongue along the back of my teeth as a distraction.

"Do you know something, Violet? Have you heard something from him?"

Oh my God, no! I wanted to scream, but I just shook my head. I am not hiding anything other than the fact that I know even less than you think. That I know nothing. Nothing! That's what all of this is: he is vanished and gone into nothing.

"You know, you could have told me he was going." Dean's voice softened. "Maybe we could have talked to him together and found out a little more about his plan."

I sobbed. A horrible bubble of air and sadness escaped from my chest.

"Violet, no. Sorry. Sorry. No. It's not your fault. Jesus, that was stupid. No. No. I shouldn't have said that." He hugged me, a little awkwardly, but his arms were tight around my shoulders. "I wasn't thinking. Really. I just miss him. You know, right? I miss him. That's all."

"I know," I said. "I know." I don't know.

It was hard to tell exactly when the hope began to shift. No one asked if we'd heard from Bliss until after a full week had gone by, which must have seemed an appropriate amount of time for him to check in.

So, at first, and for a while, my parents satisfied themselves with saying not yet, no nothing yet. But as more days passed, the looks on people's faces gradually changed as they listened to the answer. Expectation. Possibility. Hope. Uncertainty. Disappointment. Pity. Fewer dared to ask. Sometimes I saw Quinny shake her head no to an implied question that whoever she was looking at didn't dare verbalize.

The list of things I was holding in my mind to tell Bliss when he got back — that a car with a New Mexico licence plate had been in the barn parking lot (our first ever), that there was a new ice cream place open in Woodstock, that one day I'd seen Speckles at the stream and on and on — got too long, and I almost felt compelled to write things down. But I'd always think to myself, he could be back tomorrow, so why bother? Then it was the next tomorrow, then the next.

Where was he? What was he doing? Was he having fun? Was he taking pictures to show to me when he got back? Did he pause, linger, in front of a postcard rack trying to pick out the perfect one to send home? What would he write on it? Would he ever say, "Wish you were here?" I'd look at customers in our store and wonder if they could have passed by Bliss on their travels. Did they stop at the same gas station somewhere? I sometimes chose someone and imagined a little scene — Bliss coming out the door with a pop, them going in to pay for gas. Or could they have sat in the next booth over from him at a roadside restaurant? Had anyone even spoken to him? Passed him the ketchup from their table when he asked. Commented on the weather. Stood beside him at a scenic lookout and said, "Pretty view." These are the sorts of things I wondered about at the beginning.

. . .

Eventually, my parents fought. It would start the second they were back in the privacy of the house every night. The fake smiles gone. My mother blamed my father for missing the opportunity to search for Bliss when he had still been close enough to actually find.

Then one night: the Balloon Incident.

I quietly watched my mother from the stairs. I saw her take down one of the yellow balloons still hanging from the dining-room chandelier. They'd been put up for Bliss's graduation, and as days passed, then a week and now three weeks, they shrank smaller and smaller — a couple were barely the size of a lemon — but we left them there. It had been a bit of a joke, hanging them in the first place, because Mom got Bliss to blow them up himself, claiming she couldn't do it with her inferior old mom lungs.

From the stairs I saw my mother unknot the balloon with such patience and precision you'd think she was handling a priceless family heirloom. Then when she had it untied, she put the balloon to her lips and breathed in its contents. She held herself perfectly still for the longest time, and then exhaled. A single tear ran down her cheek.

I felt a pang of fear, a vibration in my chest like the effect of a loud bass note played by a church pump organ. I went upstairs as quickly as I could so Mom wouldn't hear me sob.

The next day Bliss still wasn't back. And still we waited.

And waited.

And we got sadder. And sadder.

It's been more than a year.

16

I'm going to see Foster. It's Thursday. Quinny has no problem with me going since I told her I'd be letting Foster off the hook for another trip to the Vaughn estate. I'm sure she thinks that excluding him means a greater chance of including her, as if it bumps her up the list. It's not my fault if she's misinterpreted. Cecil said that Mr. Vaughn already arranged for movers, so all I have to do is deliver the money and shake Mr. Vaughn's hand. It will only take a few minutes.

I'm inside the store choosing some books to take to Foster.

"He might like this," Dean says from behind me and pulls *The Call of the Wild* off the shelf.

"I'm fine to go alone," I say. "I know I said that you could come with me the next time, but you don't have to." I really can't ask Foster what I want if Dean is there. I take the book and put it back.

"Can't get rid of me that easy," he says.

Foster's twig art throne is empty when we get there. He's not anywhere in his yard and doesn't answer when I knock on his door. There are three new twig tables sitting near his cabin, but otherwise everything is the same as the last time I was here. Dean steps closer to Foster's big chair and runs his hand over the intricate pattern in the back.

"This thing's a masterpiece," he says.

"Violet," a voice says behind me. I startle even though I know in the same instant that it's Foster.

He's holding a dead rabbit by the ears. It's brown, long, dangling. He nods at Dean.

I hand Foster the books I picked out and tell him about the Vaughn estate.

"Fair enough," he says. "And thanks for these." He turns to go.

Dean looks at me. He starts to turn as well, but in the other direction, back towards the forest, the way we came.

"Foster, just a sec," I say. "I did want to ask you something else."

Foster stops. Waits.

I glance towards Dean.

"Over there, maybe?" I say to Foster and point at the cabin. "Dean, I won't be long."

Dean looks at Foster, at the books in one of his hands, the dead bunny in the other. "I'll be here," he says.

"You get bored you can always get started on Peter Cottontail here." Foster sets the rabbit on the ground. "My good skinning knife's over on the stump."

Dean laughs, but who knows with Foster if that was supposed to be a joke.

"Can we go inside?" I ask.

Foster answers by walking in the direction of the cabin.

We step inside. It's not any bigger than I thought it would be, although it's surprisingly cozy. It's a single room, but built into the peak of the ceiling is a sleeping loft. A ladder goes up to a platform. Above it in the ceiling is a skylight. On the platform itself is a bed, and lined against the wall is a shelf with dozens of books. Beneath the loft is a couch with an old cedar chest in front of it. In the rest of the space is a dry sink with a pitcher and basin on top, two wall-mounted kitchen cupboards, a wood stove, a small table and chair, and next to me, a large beautiful bird's-eye maple dresser. The book *Around the World in Eighty Days* is sitting on it, face down, saving his page. There are two framed pictures as well, and I pick up one of them. It's a black-and-white photo of a big beautiful two-storey house. It has six windows straight across the top floor and four plus a wide centre door on the bottom. There's a large fan-shaped window above the door. The house is white with a dark trim — likely black or green. It has two chimneys — one on each end. Lightning rods line the roof.

"This is where you grew up?" I ask.

Foster nods. "All underwater now. Except this bit of course." He taps a building in the photo's background — a dark distant rectangle.

"That's The Purple Barn?" It's hard to believe all the land between the house and the distant building.

"That's the barn," Foster says. "Didn't have its candy-coating back then — it was just old grey wood."

"Is it strange for you that it's purple now?"

"It's violet now," he says. "For you. But no, no difference to me." He smiles slightly. "Be a lot worse if your name was Dotty."

I look at the other photo. I touch my finger to the top of the frame. It's a man and woman with a boy standing between them. He's likely ten or twelve years old. All three are smiling.

"Good folks," Foster says. "Long gone now."

"Your parents? And you?"

He nods.

"Foster, do you believe in ghosts?"

"Maybe," he says. "Hard thing to know for sure."

"Have you ever seen one?"

"Is that what you wanted to ask me, Violet?"

"Could be."

Foster looks out the window to where Dean is sitting. I can see him too. He's trying out Foster's throne chair.

"I think there's lots of things on this Earth that may or may not be." He pauses. "I'm not one to doubt what anyone wants to believe."

"What do you think about the ghost herd?" I ask.

"I think it'd be quite something to see," he says.

"So you believe in it?"

He shrugs. "I don't know about some whole big herd all at once, but sure, same thing I said before. What right do I have to question the possibility?"

Foster looks out the window to Dean again. "Has he seen what you've seen?"

I shake my head. "No one said I've seen anything."

Foster nods.

The cabin is quiet.

"I have seen Speckles a couple of times lately though — down by the highway," I say.

"Sounds a little out of range for the old boy. He should be wise enough by now to stay away from it." Foster seems to study my face.

"Anyway, thanks, Foster," I say and reach for the door.

Dean and I start our walk back through the forest.

Bliss and I talked about ghosts once. It was only a couple of years ago, in October, a few weeks before Halloween. We made a little ghost-tree decoration for the store. The ghosts were made of vintage ladies' handkerchiefs with wads of tissue stuffed inside them for the heads. Mom told us to use only the plain white hankies, but we decided that adding in ones with a bit of coloured embroidery or tatted trim wouldn't hurt anything. Bliss told the story of how Barkley's little sister wanted to be a "pretty ghost" for Halloween — she'd selected a sheet with pink roses on it to wear — and could absolutely not be talked out of it.

Why were ghosts always white? Plain, just one colour, without any details? After a bit of discussion we decided it was along the lines of ghosts truly leaving their Earthly bodies behind. They changed into their simplest spirit form, a blank canvas to start fresh for whatever happened next.

Unless of course there are no ghosts — maybe there are only memories — and a ghost is something your mind makes. It is an image that's foggy, misty white, because passing time changes and dilutes all memories, adds uncertainty. Once a person is dead it is never again possible to see them clearly. They become a fading image and can never be viewed the same way as when they were alive. Ghosts then can only be blurred, fuzzy, less defined. They are imprecise and they are as light as air — steam, smoke — so they can finally float easily away.

Ghosts are only fun, silly, Halloween-costume-spooky if they're not your own. Those ghosts are like cartoon characters with three black ovals for their faces — two for eyes and one for a mouth. They go "Oooooooooh" like Dean with crazy arms. Those ghosts are the least real of all. They have no past, no connection, no meaning. Those aren't the type of ghosts that can haunt you.

We are within sight of my lawn chair at the stream edge, almost at the end of the woods before I realize I haven't said a thing to Dean and that he's let me be. But he's holding my hand. I squeeze his fingers and he squeezes back.

We head across the meadow together, back to The Purple Barn.

Dean stays outside to see if our garbage cans need emptying and I go in. Elizabeth is talking to a woman from Riverbend who Jill and I call the Curler Lady. Whenever you see her anywhere — here at the store, getting groceries, out for an evening walk around town — she always has curlers in her hair, covered with a gauzy pink scarf. If the whole idea of wearing curlers is so that your hair will look nice when it's set, who is she trying to make it look nice for? I might not even recognize her if her hair was done. I think she takes the curlers out for church maybe, so I suppose she figures God is worth impressing. I overhear her say "Vaughn cottage," and Elizabeth nods and tells her something. Then she comes over to me.

"Your father called, Violet, when you were gone," Elizabeth says. "Your parents are going to do a bit more looking around, but then they expect to be back fairly soon. And your dad wants you to do another quick check on the house."

Pepper Shaker is at my feet, circling my legs.

"Okay," I say as I bend to pick him up.

"Your dad sounded happy," Elizabeth says. "I think the vacation must have been good for them, but it'll be nice to have them back, won't it?"

"Yeah," I say. I kiss Pepper Shaker on the head.

I am hoping everything will be better when we're together again.

I stay until five o'clock, then Dean and I go to the house. Nothing is any different inside. I open the patio door to circulate some air. The lawn is probably six inches high so I send Dean out with the mower. It doesn't take him long. We go over to the Irving Restaurant to eat. At the campsite, we get some ice cream for dessert at The Snack Shack. Dwayne tells us that our neighbour Ivan Longwood checked out, and I'm a little disappointed we didn't get a chance to talk to him again, or at least say goodbye. Dean and I sit together on the porch in the rocking chairs. Jill is inside crocheting a doily. Johnny stops in for a minute after a shopping trip to Fredericton. He takes Dean back to Riverbend, and I head in to bed.

It's only when I'm lying there that I let myself think about what Foster said. About ghosts — and possibilities.

I wonder what the ghost deer wants with me.

17

It's just before nine in the morning, another sunny day, and as I round the corner of the barn, Quinny's blue Ford LTD pulls in. Her husband George is driving and he parks at the other end of the lot. They both get out and George goes around to Quinny's side. For a second it looks as if they might kiss goodbye, but I don't see George duck under the inner tube of her hair to do it. Instead he opens the back passenger side door. He takes out a yellow quilt. He passes it to Quinny, who holds her arms out in front of her so he can set if flat. He smooths a wrinkle from the top of it, then evens the folded edges.

The quilt is a pattern of rows and rows of triangles. Right-angle triangles, as I remember them being called in math class, so I bet George likes the calculated symmetry of the pattern. I stop and watch as George smooths the quilt again, then picks a little thread off it. He checks the other side. He does it carefully. So carefully.

I go back around the corner of the barn out of sight and wait as Quinny goes inside and George leaves. Dean comes up quietly behind me.

"Who you hiding from?" he asks. Then he steps ahead and scans the empty parking lot. "I'd say the coast is clear."

"I was thinking for a minute," I say. "I might have figured something out."

"Why it is you find me so irresistible?"

I give him a little shove.

Dean and I are leaving early because it's Johnny's birthday and he wants us to go out to supper with Jill and him. I search through our massive shelf of books in the store and choose a 1925 Ford car repair manual to give Johnny as a gift.

Then I go to Quinny. She's alone at the cash reading a *Family Circle* magazine.

"Good, Violet," she says when she sees me approaching. "I must talk to you about your trip to the Vaughn estate tomorrow."

"Okay," I say.

"I've already arranged with Elizabeth for her to come in early so I can go with you."

"Oh," I say. "Well, there's really no need. Cecil will be there and it will just take a few minutes to hand over the cash. Thanks anyway, though."

She pinches her lips together and inhales the tiniest sniff. I wonder if she really thinks I can't see through her. If she'd admit that she's insanely desperate to see the place, rather than pretending to help me, I'd feel less annoyed about the whole thing.

"No," she says. "I really don't think that will suffice. I've already made the arrangements. And I think it would be best if I drove, so we can take the car and leave from here."

I don't say anything right away. I slowly scan the store, as if considering what Quinny's said, surveying the inventory, customers, then I lift my eyes to the quilt that is hanging from the rafters above us. It has perfect points, beautiful geometry. Meticulously measured, mathematically calculated and executed with precision — really not anything that could be produced quickly by only working a few hours each evening. I took home ec in grade nine, and I've seen my mother sew curtains, a dress now and then and my Halloween costumes over the years. No matter how much of a craftswoman extraordinaire Quinny makes herself out to be, a sewing machine only runs so fast.

"George won't need the car tomorrow?" I ask. "To buy fabric or anything?"

"Oh no," she says. "It's all arranged and I'm well stocked."

"I meant does George need any fabric."

Quinny's lips purse and she says, "Violet, I hardly have time for silly games now. The store is busy." She looks around quickly, checking that no one is close enough to have overheard my questions.

If I wasn't already sure before, I would be now. And it does make sense. George's quilts are a mathematician's masterpieces.

"George is very tal —"

"Very well then, Violet, that's enough. Go ahead yourself tomorrow. But now it's so busy, I must get back."

There might be six customers in the store.

Quinny spins around and rushes away. She wipes her hands on her skirt as she goes.

That was easier than I figured. I only intended the quilt conversation as a diversion until I thought of some other way to disappoint her about the Vaughn estate, not as a threat that I was going to expose some secret. The business of the quilts is between her and George.

But I do wonder how it came to be that Quinny takes the credit. Was it her idea? George's? Sure a lot of men wouldn't be caught dead sitting at a sewing machine, so is it that? Worrying what people will think? Did someone just assume once that Quinny was the quilter, and they were too embarrassed to set the record straight? (My mother said once that Quinny and George couldn't have any children. And that made Quinny abrupt and matter of fact, and maybe it could have been different — or at least having kids may have softened her up.) She doesn't seem too pleased that I know though. She's at the far end of the barn now, loudly rearranging a display of wooden pop crates, and I wonder if she could be coming unstitched, slightly ripping apart at the seams.

Jill made us reservations for the birthday supper at the restaurant in the King's Head Inn at the Landing. The restaurant serves traditional New Brunswick homestyle cooking. The waitresses wear the old costumes like Jill does and the rooms are lit with candles. (Once an unaware tourist leaned against a lit wall sconce and singed her ponytail.)

Jill and Johnny are already seated when Dean and I arrive. They're in one of the smaller more private dining rooms, at a table in the corner. They're holding hands across the table and leaning in towards each other. I feel like a romantic-moment wrecker, and I know Dean and I were only invited because of Jill's commitment to keeping me entertained this summer.

Dean says, "Hey, old man!" before we're barely through the entry of the room.

"Well there we go, glad you're here," Johnny says.

"The big two-o," Dean says, "and still hanging with us teenagers."

"Wouldn't have it any other way," Johnny says. "Can't get a better babysitter than me." He grins.

We sit down. The waitress in her long skirt, blouse, apron and tidy little white bonnet is taking our order within a few minutes.

We all get the same thing — a turkey dinner. For dessert we have gingerbread with a heaping blob of whipped cream. It's either that or apple pie. The waitress brings Johnny's out with a lit candle in it and we sing for him. He opens his presents — the car manual from me, a bottle of Jack Daniel's from Dean and an ABBA eight-track from Jill.

But then he surprises all three of us by standing up.

"Speech! Speech!" Dean says.

"Now, now, now, let's keep 'er calm," Johnny says. Then he cocks his head subtly, his chin angling slightly towards Jill, just so, while still looking at Dean.

Johnny clears his throat.

I look at Jill. She sits up straighter in her seat. She reaches for her glass and takes a quick sip of water.

"All right," Johnny says. "With this being my birthday, I thought I'd give myself a little present too, a very special one-of-a-kind gift."

In seconds Johnny is around to Jill's side and down on one knee. He pulls a silver dome-shaped Birks ring box out of his back pocket. A tear is already running down Jill's cheek.

"Jill," he says and takes her hand, "more than anything I want you by my side forever. That would be the best gift of all. Will you marry me?"

"Yes, yes, of course, yes," she says. Then she starts sobbing. The ring goes on her finger. She is frozen in place for a few seconds staring at her ring as if trying to count how many times her reflection appears in the many facets. Then she lunges for Johnny and they hug.

She hugs me next. "Vi, oh my God, oh my God, oh my God," she whispers in my ear. "I did it. I'm engaged. I'm really engaged. I did it." She is still crying.

"You did it," I whisper back.

That easy. Joy. Excitement. The start of something. The beginning of happily ever after. Then I am crying too.

Bliss did bring up the boneyard in conversation, for the first time in years, not long before he left. We were at the barn planting the new marigolds for the season around the bottom of our big sign. We'd stopped by after school. It was the last week of May so the store didn't have much tourist traffic yet, but a few people pulled in and out of the parking lot as we worked.

When we were almost done, two men stopped to talk to us. They were both wearing coveralls. They'd come from the store and were each drinking a bottle of Coke.

"Looking good," one said. "Gonna be doing the same thing ourselves upriver soon enough." He turned and gestured to his truck that was across the parking lot. It was filled with trays of flowers in the back, along with rakes and shovels. There was also a lawn mower and a large metal garbage can marked "Province of New Brunswick." The two men were the Undertakers.

I looked at Bliss. I knew he knew too.

"So you got any tips?" the man said.

"Probably just to give them a good drink after," Bliss said. "That's what we were told, right, Vi?"

I nodded.

"Well have a good one then," the Undertaker said.

I watched the two men walk across the parking lot to their truck. Then they flipped down the tailgate and sat and lit cigarettes.

I wasn't quite sure what to say, if I should just pretend we hadn't seen them, but Bliss spoke first.

"Did you ever think about it, Vi, what the chances were? I mean out of this whole stretch of highway and all this forest, the boneyard ended up back there?"

I shook my head. I didn't know how to respond.

"You know, a nice sunny day like today, I'm feeling good, relaxed, and I can forget about it, tell myself different about it, but I know it's still back there waiting. I know it'll come back on me again."

I nodded. The thing was, that part of it I did know. As clearly as I knew that the boneyard was near us here and now, in our forest, it was always near Bliss. The boneyard had become a self-fulfilling prophecy for him. It had become one with the darkness that he couldn't escape. The boneyard had built in his mind, tightened its grip with each remembering, so that trying to purge it completely from his memory had become as hard as forgetting his own name.

"You know it's never going to leave me, Vi," he said.

Bliss looked at me, and all the things I had thought about, all the questions that had accumulated in the years he had kept me on the outside of his sorrow, came to me at once. Mostly, why? Why did this happen? Why Bliss? Why did his brain betray him like this? And why not mine, why not Mom's or Dad's? What were those chances? Where had it come from? Was it a fluke — like Speckles's fur? Or was it something passed on? Was it something like this that had made my great-uncle drink, made him "not right" after the war? This was so unfair. Bliss was so good, so kind. And yet he went through this ever-returning torture when his own mind could make him forget how wonderful he really was, convince him he had always been wrong about himself.

"What if you left it?" The words slipped from my mouth.

And of course I meant only mind over matter, for him to try to think differently. Same as I always suggested when we used to talk about it. That's it — because I could never completely understand what he felt — that's it, that's all I meant. Really, that's it, nothing more.

A month later he was gone.

I don't know why I wake. Was there a sound? The tiny cottage bedroom is quiet and dark. The curtain hangs perfectly straight in front of the open window. There's no breeze, not the slightest shift of its fabric. Dean is lying beside me. I can't even hear him breathing, but as my eyes adjust to the dark I can tell that the sheet covering him is ever so slightly rising and falling. It's just the two of us. Johnny and Jill aren't here; they're at Johnny's parents' place for the weekend, since his parents are away. I sit up slowly. I listen. Nothing. Then the distant sound of a truck passing by on the highway. Then nothing again.

But I had woken with a start. I'd been dreaming of Bliss. We were running around in the field behind the barn, then suddenly I wasn't anymore. I cuddle up to Dean, put my head on his chest. Close my eyes again.

This time the sound is subtle. Not enough to wake me if I were asleep. Is it a scratching? A branch rubbing slightly against the window in the breeze? A squirrel on the roof? A bird picking bugs from the dead leaves in the rain gutters? Not at night. The sound is coming from the side of the cottage.

I slide away from Dean as quietly as I can. I take the three steps to the open window. I realize it's probably a moth batting its wings against the screen. I move back the curtain and sure enough, I catch dark wings flitting away. The campground is especially dark. Dwayne finally took the Christmas lights down, and the pool lights are off. The sky is overcast as well, no moon or stars.

The air at the window is cool, and now that I'm completely awake I stand in it. I take a few deep breaths. I turn to go back to bed when I catch the slightest glow of light, as if someone has turned on a lamp in the next cottage — except I know it's vacant. I lean ahead but I can't quite see the source of it at this angle.

Then the scratching sound starts again. And I'm sure it isn't — wasn't — a moth. I look out because I can't help myself and the light seems to have become slightly brighter. There is something at the edge of my vision. It is a white thigh, leg, and cloven hoof.

The ghost deer.

So close. Right there.

I jump back and bang into the edge of the bed, then fall sideways onto the end of it. Dean shifts in his sleep, rolls over, but doesn't wake.

I look down at the sheet underneath me. The way my heart is beating, I almost expect to see it rippling from the vibration. Dean doesn't move.

I stare at him lying there. I could crawl in bed beside him, tuck myself under his arm and go to sleep again.

Instead I pick my shorts up off the floor and pull them on. I slip my sandals on at the front door and head outside.

I go down the porch steps, walk along the side of the truck in the driveway and stop at the corner of the cottage.

I take a step and stop again. Nothing yet. Then I move along the back of the cottage. It does feel a bit cooler though, and I get a chill. Or it could be a cold flood of relief that there's nothing out here. That I can go inside and get in bed with Dean.

But I see a slight brightness ahead. I am barely aware of it before the buck steps out. Solid and white, but phosphorescent. With its movement a blast of air as cold as January. A winter breath. It's ten feet away. I gasp and cough, then fall back against the cottage.

The buck doesn't startle. It looks at me, waits, turns away and walks, saunters, slowly in the direction of the rest of the campground, then eventually the highway.

I watch it go.

"Speckles?" I finally manage to squeak out. But it is out of sight behind trees and gone.

It wasn't Speckles. Even hearing myself say his name, trying to pretend, trying to forget what I've already had to accept makes me feel worse.

I hurry to follow the buck. There are no campsites where he walked, just trees. It's hard to see in the dark, to trace the exact path he took. It's as if he has suddenly vanished. The air feels even, warm. Not a trace of cool breeze. I look for a glow. But there's nothing. Except the distant headlights of a vehicle way up on the highway.

I should go back. Forget it.

I could turn around.

But then the buck is there, ahead, stepping from behind a tree, climbing the last little bit of slope that leads to the highway.

I feel such a pull to it. To see if its feet are actually touching the ground. I start running as fast as I can.

It hears me. Turns to look back.

Then it darts, leaps, bounds up towards the highway. I know I have startled it, chased it, forced it to go.

And the headlights are coming so close now. Big lights, tall lights. A truck. In three bounds the deer is to the shoulder of the road.

I can't help but keep running. I have to see.

In another single bound the buck is in one lane.

I stop. A blur of light. The long loud blare of a transport's horn. For a second I can't breathe. But I am still, and so scared, that I have complete focus. I can see clearly in the beams of the truck's headlights, and there is nothing there.

I run and as sickening as it is, I listen for a thud, a snap, something being hit and thrown. But I don't hear it. The sound of the truck gets more distant. Then the silence of the night returns.

Until Dean's voice.

"Vi! Vi! Violet! Are you out here? Violet?!" He sounds frantic. "Violet!" I can hear him coming. I hear the sound of a tree branch bend then spring back. I hear him trip. Scramble back up. "Violet! Violet! Can you hear me?"

"Dean," I finally say. He's already at my side.

"Oh my God," he says. He hugs me. Presses my arms into my sides. He is breathing hard. "Oh my God, why are you up here? I heard the horn and the truck and Jesus Christ, Violet, why were you on the highway?" He pulls back and stares at me but his hands are still on my shoulders. "You can't be on the highway!"

I turn cold again.

"I wasn't on the highway," I say. My voice is surprisingly even.

"I heard the horn. Violet, what in hell are you doing up here?" He is scared. His eyes are dark.

"I wasn't on the highway."

"You have to tell me what you're doing up here. My God, Violet, it's the middle of the night. We were sound asleep in bed and now you're up here, standing on the shoulder, and I heard the truck go by and that wasn't a friendly beep hello. You're scaring the shit out of me. Look, Violet, I'm here. I'm listening. What are you doing? You have to tell me."

"There was a ghost deer."

Dean shakes his head. "No, Vi. No! We can't do this now. You have to be serious. You can't joke this time."

"What if I'm not joking?" I don't know what else to say.

"Oh my God, Vi, don't. There was no — wait — did you have a nightmare? Were you sleepwalking?" He tightens his grip on my shoulders and shakes me slightly.

"Quit it. I wasn't sleepwalking."

A car passes by in the opposite lane. Its lights wash over us. The slight breeze from it blows my hair. Dean hasn't taken his eyes off me.

"Vi?" His voice is insistent.

"Speckles," I say. "Okay?"

"Where, Vi? You were asleep inside the cottage."

"I woke up and he was outside."

No response.

"And I knew he shouldn't be down here. So I went out to look. And then he ran off and I followed him — up here. That's it. Speckles, okay?"

"Bliss's deer — the one he used to talk about?"

"Yes."

"Speckles," he says.

Dean looks around. I don't know what's he's thinking.

"The night we went to Old Home Week too, Vi? It was Speckles you thought you saw then?"

"Yeah," I say.

Dean blows out a long even breath.

"And he went back to the forest, I take it?" he asks. "He's gone now?"

"He's gone now."

"Come back with me then," Dean says and takes my hand.

I look across the highway one more time. There's nothing there.

We go back to the cottage.

We lie in bed awake, not talking, for what seems like forever.

"You know, no matter what you think, Vi, how you twist it, it wasn't your responsibility," Dean finally says. "You wouldn't have been able to stop him anyway."

"But I needed to try. You must understand that, right? That I needed to try?"

"Yeah," he says. "I get that."

And we could've been talking about the deer.

Or we could have been talking about Bliss.

18

It's late morning when I finally decide to get up on Saturday, but I still have plenty of time before I head to the Vaughn estate. Dean is long gone to the barn. We talked briefly when he first woke though, and he had me promise that I'd stay at the house in Riverbend tonight—away from the deer and the highway. Just to be on the safe side, he said.

After I shower, I choose a floral halter top, shorts and sandals. I go to The Snack Shack. Dwayne's busy giving driving directions to an older couple. There's a big camper outside with a white-and-red Wisconsin licence plate that says "America's Dairyland," which I bet is theirs. Dwayne has a New Brunswick map spread on the counter. I choose a Pepsi, pull open the tab and connect it to his sparkling chain, grab a Wigwag chocolate bar and a bag of Humpty Dumpty chips. I slide a two dollar bill across the counter to him on my way out.

There are cars parked along the shoulder of Pine Lake Road almost a quarter mile before the public beach at the end. They're backed up well past the canteen parking lot and the entry to the campsite. I drive slowly, squeezing the truck between the cars, approaching vehicles and a few people walking, damp towels flung over their shoulders. It's a beautiful day for swimming or sitting at the lake's edge. The sun is reflecting bright and shiny on the side-view mirrors and chrome bumpers.

I turn and drive quickly down the road through the trees, past the winding cottage driveways to the part where the road turns wild. Then I slow down, and roll up the windows so I won't get hit by passing tree branches. The road is every bit as bumpy as I remember, but it seems shorter than last time now that I've been down it once before. Cecil is sitting on the tailgate of his truck waiting. It's the only vehicle here. He jumps down and comes over to me as I park.

"Miss Violet," he says. "Beautiful day."

"It is. You still alone?" I ask.

"Alone here. Mr. Vaughn's inside already. I'll take you right in."

At the house Cecil holds the front door open for me. I step into the large open room. It's as wonderful as I remember.

A man's voice startles me.

"Violet Davis," he says.

"Mr. Vaughn," I start. I turn and he's sitting at the long dining table. But it isn't a Mr. Vaughn. It's Ivan Longwood.

"It's you," I say.

"You know Mr. Vaughn already?" Cecil asks, confused.

"Cecil, you know you can call me Ivan," he says. "And yes, just a coincidence, but I met Violet not too long ago."

"Well, good enough then," Cecil says. "Now I'll be outside having a smoke until you're done," he says. "Let me know if you need anything."

Cecil leaves, and I sit at the table across from Ivan.

"I thought you said your name was Ivan Longwood," I say.

"It is," he says. "Ivan Longwood Vaughn. Everything I told you and your friends was the truth. About university, about looking around down here this summer. And this is the place I've been landscaping, cleaning up the yard a bit before it's sold. I left off my last name because my mother suggested I shouldn't use it down here, in case it caused some curiosity. Keep a low profile, you know. I suppose I might have had people asking me about selling the place and I really wanted no hassle with that — just wanted to leave it to the lawyer."

"Did you know who I was?"

"It did click after I was introduced. But it surprised me. You're so young and you were staying at the campsite. But I'm glad I met you. And I'm glad you're buying the things. Up until then, I would've just agreed to let the lawyer sell it all along with the land and house — made no difference to me. I only told him no after I talked to you. You made me change my mind."

"Really?"

"Yeah. It just seems right that all this goes to your place somehow."

"Thanks. I know a lot of people will like to see everything that's in here. People remember Ivy well. She was your grandmother?"

"Yes."

"Her rainbow room is something else. I've never seen anything like it. I'm actually planning to put all her glass on display in the store's booth at our Community Days. I know people will love it."

"See, I knew I chose right. Her rainbow room is really the only thing I remember from when I was a kid."

"How old were you the last time you were here?"

"Six."

"That's a long time ago," I say.

"But you know the story of the place, right? Why we left?"

"A boy drowned. One of your relatives."

"Kevin Vaughn. He was sixteen. Fell out of a boat."

"I'm sorry," I say. "I heard he was swimming to rescue someone."

"Well, he was trying to rescue someone. Or I guess he thought he was. He'd come after me."

I feel a prickle in my chest.

"He was my cousin," Ivan says.

"I'm so sorry," I say again. "I didn't know."

"It was a long time ago," Ivan says, looks down.

I move a little in my chair and the old wood creaks.

"I had taken the boat out myself, which I'm sure I shouldn't have. But I bet I would have come back to shore eventually. We were across the lake having a picnic. Mom and my aunt started freaking out, yelling at me, and I guess I ignored them. I was six. I was just being a kid. I don't remember. But Kevin was there and took it upon himself to swim out to me, a long way, even though he wasn't a strong swimmer. When he's all the way out he's near exhausted, and then he slips and hits his head on the boat trying to pull himself in."

I nod and look past him out the window. I focus on the tiniest bit of water that I can see through the trees.

"You know it's not your fault," I say.

"I know that now. I wanted to jump out of the boat after him. But Mom and my aunt screamed and screamed not to move, so I stayed put. Which now I know might have saved me from drowning too. Dad and my uncle rushed in from down the beach and swam out, but it was too late."

"Is it hard being back here?" I ask.

"No." A pause. "Okay, it was at first. Actually that first day I saw you at the campsite — in the canteen — was right after I'd been down here for the first time. It did come back. There were memories waiting for me here. But after a bit, no. No, what happened was a long time ago. Mom suggested I come here and take care of it all for everyone. Put it all away. This place. But what happened is long gone for me."

We are both quiet for several seconds.

I slide the envelope of cash that is sitting between us on the table a little bit towards him. He lays his hand flat on top of it, pats it twice.

"Violet, you know what? You can't be responsible for the decisions other people make. I can't blame myself for what my cousin did. I have gone through it in my mind so many times, wondering about every other possible way it could have turned out. But you can't know or control other people's thoughts. You can't always stop them from doing what they want."

"Yeah."

"So anyway, my family's letting the place go. It was my grandmother's dream, so many of her best memories are here, and if people who knew her or remember her want to buy what was in the house, that's great. What happened with Kevin was a tragedy, but the fun times he had here are with us too. There are many, many good things here, family memories. Like you mentioned the rainbow room. I'm so glad I saw it again. My grandmother was a wonderful person. I could almost feel her presence in there. That's what I think my parents hoped I would realize, sending me down here. Life goes on."

I nod.

"And Violet, my sincere condolences about your brother."

"You know about Bliss?"

"That was his name? I haven't heard that before. The Mrs. Quinn who spoke to my mother on the phone mentioned him. Mom thought the business was called Charles J. Davis and Son, so when Mrs. Quinn said it would be a daughter coming, she asked where the son was. Just a simple question. She had no idea."

I nod. "Thanks."

"He must have died quite young, if you don't mind me asking?"

"He was eighteen," I say. "He died last year. A year tomorrow actually. It was an accident too."

Ivan shakes his head. "I'm so sorry."

Cecil knocks twice on the side of the screen door then comes back in. "All set, Violet?"

I look up at Cecil then over at Ivan.

"May I go in the rainbow room again?" I ask.

"Absolutely," Ivan says and gestures towards it.

. . .

I walk to the middle of the floor. The mid-afternoon sun is perfect. There are dots of coloured light on my arms, my legs, the walls. I start to spin myself, squint my eyes. Colours blur. I do see the rainbow. The sunset. The sunrise. Fireworks. The lit-up rides at Old Home Week. Birthday candles. The police car flashing red and blue in the Canada Day parade. A field party bonfire. A meteor shower. The tree plugged in on Christmas morning. The Northern Lights. I am dizzy but it doesn't matter. I spin and spin then sit perfectly still until it goes away, all of it, at least for now.

I go back out and shake Ivan's hand. "Thanks," I say. "For everything."

19

I'm alone in Bliss's room. I'm sitting on the end of his bed. His room as he left it. Clothes in the closet, graduation cap beside me on the pillow. I've been in here a long time, hours and hours, since I came back from the Vaughn estate. I phoned Dean and told him I'd rather just stay here by myself.

But I've decided I'm going to go. I have to know.

It's finally dark, a little after nine. I get in the truck and drive to the barn. Park around back. Walk the path through the meadow to the woods. I don't have a flashlight, it's just me and the moon. There are sounds from the highway, but nothing from the woods. I step under the cover of trees and sit in my lawn chair at the stream. Wait. I'm not fearful this time. I'm confident. I believe the white buck will come.

I wait. And wait.

The air is surprisingly warm, but the day was so hot it will likely take until morning for the heat to completely dissipate. The highway is still loud with summer traffic, big trucks rumbling along, making up for the delayed miles they endured behind campers and station wagons pulling trailers. The headlights are distant streaks in my periphery. Someone drives by with their windows down, and I can hear the radio or eight-track player, even voices carrying in the breeze. Faint sounds drift up from the campsite too — talk and laughter. I turn to see if I can hear people jumping in the pool, the splashes echoing. It's hard to tell.

But then I feel a change in the air. An expanding cold chill. And from nowhere, a glow like the moon has dropped from the sky to the ground right beside me. I know the deer is there now, and I have to look.

The white buck stands as still as in a painting, not even ten feet in front of me. It is shining, but it also looks solid and sleek. I can see the texture of its fur. It is muscular and tall. In my chair I'm only to its thighs. Its antlers are full, polished bone with so many dangerously sharp tips.

I draw in a breath to steady myself, scared I will startle it away. It tilts its head ever so slightly and I see its antlers pass right through a branch without it moving or springing back. I shift in my chair and pull up my knees to rub my legs.

The deer doesn't dart but nods its head, bends it deep in front of me. Its red eyes seem to soften. When I push off my chair, as slowly as I can, the buck jerks its head up and steps back. Its nostrils seem to flare, but there's no snort, no sound. No breath.

It turns to go and I am compelled to follow. The buck leaves an illuminated beam in its trail. The forest is like a solid black wall around me, and I can see only in the narrow path the deer takes. Every few hundred feet it stops and turns as if to check that I'm still coming.

We walk back into the woods, moving away from the stream, deeper into the forest, surely well beyond the boneyard, and beyond Foster's cabin. The sounds of the highway and the campsite are gone. Still it leads me on.

I trip more than once on tree roots, and while staying so carefully in the buck's trail of light, I walk through alders and underbrush. Low branches scrape and scratch me. The buck never seems to waiver or have to step over or around anything, yet it doesn't float, it walks. I see it take step after step, cloven hooves on the ground. I would like to sit on a rock to rest, but I don't. I need to keep up with the buck.

The deer finally stops and turns to me again before glancing off to the side. In the darkness, where we are doesn't look any different than the rest of the forest we've just passed through. There are still trees and more trees, tall black trunks and shadowy branches. The buck turns and walks two steps and disappears. The trail of light vanishes for a second. Then, rising up from just beyond where it had stood is the bright glow of snow that exists in a whiteout, like a luminescent fog.

We have somehow circled to the boneyard. I am sure of it, even though it feels far from where I've ever been before.

I go to the edge of the slope in front of me and stop. I grab a tree branch to help steady myself. A wide tall beam of light illuminates the pit.

Below is the ghost herd. But I'm not scared; I feel almost serene. They are beautiful when they are all together. It has to be the whole herd — there are hundreds of them. Moose and deer, bucks, does, fawns and calves all glowing with a soft white light. Their heads are lowered as if they are grazing, unaware of me. They seem peaceful.

The white buck that led me here is still standing at the edge of the pit, high above the others. It looks over at me with glowing red eyes. Snorts. It's a distinct sound that I can hear this time. Then every head of the white herd raises. The beauty of the scene dissipates. As the animals lift their glowing highway eyes to me, one by one, the translucent glow of the animals is shot through with red dots — and in such quick succession that the colour spreads across the white mass like a blood spatter.

I scream.

I scream like I have never screamed in my life, and as the sound leaves my body the white buck locks eyes with me, nods, then leaps — purposefully, directly — into the mass of the white animals below. When he lands they begin to shatter like glass. But it isn't shards that fall to the ground, it's bones. White bones that pile up. The sound of it is terrible, smashing and breaking and clattering together as they land. And after, bouncing off all the trees in the forest, are the echoes of screeching tires and blaring horns, awful thuds and the crush and crunch of metal.

Within seconds, half of the deer and moose are gone and replaced by bones, piling up, covering the ground. The deer are cracking and shattering, and as each one breaks the pit is getting darker. The bones don't glow on their own the way the fully formed animals did. I can't stand the sound so I turn and run. And run. I make it a long way before I hit a tree, smash into it with my cheek and forehead in the pitch-black. I fall, fast, and so heavy and hard. Then I lie still on the forest floor, trying to catch my breath, laying my cheek against damp leaves. It feels instantly bruised, scraped and stinging. Everything is dark in front of me, but it seems the air is spinning. I bring up my knees, roll into some underbrush and I am out.

When I wake the first time it's still dark. It seems there are leaves covering my eyes and I'm lying on a whole tangle of tree roots, hard and criss-crossed. My back hurts. My forehead and cheek throb and I feel woozy and confused. I drift off again.

When I wake next it's daylight. Above me are overlapping evergreen branches and the tall trunk of a leaning trembling aspen. In the open spaces in between, the sun is taking over the whole sky. I push myself to stand. My whole body feels weak. My head hurts. My cheek hurts. I walk ten paces to a rotting tree and sit back down, propping myself against it. I'm in a section of woods I haven't seen before. (It's not as if I have the whole place memorized, and certainly a lot of it looks the same, but I know.) There are tamaracks here. Pines, spruces, a rotting tree trunk, ferns, mosses, rocks, lots of rocks. Leaves are blown across the forest floor from the aspen.

I listen for anything familiar like the trucks on the highway, the gurgling of the stream, the crows by the boneyard. At first I can only hear the creak and squeak of branches in the slightest breeze, but the crows might be there too, cawing, in the distance.

I know better than to walk aimlessly in the woods. My current situation may not be the best evidence of that, but I do know. If I'm really lost I shouldn't move. If I'm not a hundred per cent sure how to get back, I should wait. But it's Sunday, and the store isn't open today. No one will have missed me. Dean thinks I slept at the house. Jill and Johnny are at his parents' place. My parents are away.

And my brother is gone.

I listen again: a red squirrel or chipmunk in a tree, a falling cone, no stream, no traffic, but the crows are there, faintly. I really do think it's them.

I get up and walk the best I can towards the sound of the cawing. I come to a spot where it looks like I may have been last night — a place that looks disturbed and trampled down. Ferns are squished and broken and branches of underbrush are snapped and bent. As I turn in a circle to take in my surroundings, I get disoriented, so I can't tell anymore where I came in. I sit on the ground. The quiet of the forest is awful.

"Foster!"

"Foster!" I yell as loudly as I can. I tilt my head back and put my hands on each side of my mouth to help project the sound. "Foster, it's Violet!"

I listen. Nothing.

"Foster! Can you hear me?"

"Foster! Foster!"

No response.

I must yell his name twenty more times at least. I yell and yell until my throat is sore.

I'm lost in the woods.

I lie flat on the ground. My legs are tired and burning, with dampness and dirt in all the scratches from the underbrush. There are pine needles in my sandals, the mulch and sludge of dead leaves crammed under my toenails, and the straps have rubbed red lines across the bridge of my feet. Around me it's all trees. Close trees block distant trees. Branches and leaves in the foreground block branches and leaves in the background.

I wonder what time it is. Could it be noon yet?

"Foster! It's Violet!"

And once the slight echo of my voice completely fades, there is no other sound. No reply, no distant movement. Not even cawing anymore. Nothing.

I don't know what to do. Time passes. Perhaps an hour of indecision.

I finally roll onto my side. More trees and underbrush fill my view. Not just branches now but trunks, fat and thin. And there is something else too, at the edge of what my vision can make out. Far away, near the base of a large tree is a slightly rounded brown form. It's a groundhog maybe? A rabbit?

"Hey!" I yell to see if it will move. But it's really far away. "Hey!" I repeat and clap my hands. Nothing happens.

I stand and walk towards the brown form. I don't try to be quiet, and whatever it is doesn't move from my noise anyway. Something inanimate?

No. Brown fur. I am close enough now that I can tell.

I walk on and realize what I saw is the tiniest bit of the back end of a deer. I can make out its brown tail, the white underside showing at the edges.

It's odd it hasn't startled.

. . .

I can see more and more of it as I gradually approach, and when its back comes into view, the brown fur turns out to be just a splotch against a torso of white. Then with the little I see of its back legs, I can see white. The bits of brown are splashes and dots. It's Speckles. That's why he didn't startle. Speckles is different. Speckles is gentle and knows me.

I walk faster. At this point it feels as if I've found a friend, and all the annoyances of sore throat, tired scratched legs, thirst, hunger and headache seem to diminish.

I am almost to him.

But then there is a whisper in the trees, the branches bend and leaves twist in a breeze. Something is blown my way.

The sick sour stench of sadness.

Speckles is dead.

My stomach clenches and pushes a horrible pressure up through my chest, my throat, my mouth that comes out as a sob. I gasp in a huge breath and sob again. Poor Speckles. I cry and feel the urge to reach out to him, to lean in and hug him, but I don't move any closer. There are things I won't dwell on, details of the deteriorating condition of his body, but I can tell he's been dead a while. He's been lying here more than just a day — maybe weeks. I don't know enough to tell for sure. What I do know is that he's long gone. At least I'm going to assume it wasn't a dramatic ending. He died of old age. He lay down beneath the tree, his job here done.

I wipe away my tears.

I stare until I am calm again, thinking of the time Bliss asked Speckles if he'd be his deer, his pet.

And now Speckles is gone too. He is not here in this rotting carcass, his sweet soul has lifted and floated away. Beautiful Speckles would be flawless in death. His brown splotches would be gone in his spirit form. Speckles would be all white now. Plain, snowy white.

A ghost? A ghost.

Like Bliss and I talked about once.

I drop to my knees.

It could make sense. It could make perfect sense. It *was* Speckles I saw these few weeks, coming for me, wanting to see me, trying to tell me something. "Hey, Speckles, check in with me and Vi here, let us know you're doing okay," Bliss had said that first day we met him. That's what Speckles was doing — what the ghost deer was doing. The Speckles I saw was a ghost.

"Was it you?" I whisper.

"It was you, wasn't it?"

Maybe this is what sadness does to you. Opens you up to other things. It makes your mind work in new ways to attempt to overcome the fact that so much of it is taken up with despair. Is it your mind that creates ghosts, needs ghosts? Lets you figure out what you need? Lets you believe what you need to believe? Is that how it works?

I say goodbye to Speckles and walk away.

It's no less sad that he's dead, but at least he's up here, and not mangled and strewn in the boneyard. It's a small mercy.

And now I am determined it will be the boneyard that saves me.

I can hear the crows again, faintly in the distance. I close my eyes to listen better, to concentrate only on the sound. I walk towards it over rocks and fallen logs. To keep my path true, I carefully count my paces to the right or left to go around a tree, so I can be sure to go the exact amount back again.

I stop and wait until I can clearly hear the cawing again. I know it is getting louder. I walk. Ignore the pain in my legs and in my head. Try not to think about how horribly dry my mouth is. I have been in this forest before. Dozens of times. Maybe not this exact spot, but these trees are relatives — cousins — of the trees I know. The crows are the same ones I always hear.

I eventually find the slight slope, and though I've approached from a completely different direction than before, I know I'm at the boneyard. The horrible familiar smell of it. And if I step to the edge of the boneyard, then I can circle the perimeter to the entry point I remember, trace my way back to the stream, then The Purple Barn.

I walk ahead and there's an enormous pit. The side of it drops straight down. I grab a tree branch and squeeze my eyes tight for a second to stop the dizziness. The boneyard is bigger than I've ever seen. It is vast, almost endless, filled with things I didn't want to think of anymore.

The place I'd looked at it from before, the spot that Bliss and I arrived at that very first day we saw it, is a little tiny thumb that sticks out the far side, partially blocked by trees. The full boneyard is probably ten times bigger than we had ever known. That was how I had walked so far last night and still ended up here.

Following Speckles. This is where he brought me.

A feeling comes over me, a wash of fear and sadness and I stand frozen. Tears run down my cheeks. Bliss's deer. Speckles. The ghost deer. The white hart. He waited for me. He snorted so I would look at him and then he showed me what he had wanted to all along. He didn't step by accident over the cliff. He *leapt*. On purpose. That was what I have to accept and believe. That was the end.

I cry the way I should have cried so many times already. The crows are scared off and pass over me like a black cloud, blocking the sun. A dark shadow forms then lifts away. I sob and wail until there are two hands around my waist.

"Vi," Dean says. "I got you. I got you."

I hug him tight. I bury my head in his neck, and I catch a glimpse of Foster standing behind him.

"I was coming back," I say. "I didn't want to leave. I wasn't taking off. I was coming back. I was. I wouldn't leave. I wouldn't."

"I know."

Dean leads me out of the forest.

20

My parents didn't go to find Bliss. They knew he wasn't there.

Police officers came to our door a long time ago, just short of a month after Bliss had left. The few sentences they spoke were enough to crumple my mother to the floor.

Bliss would not return, but be returned to us.

They went to find a memory of him. They went to find one person who had been where Bliss had been and remembered him. Someone who he had seen, talked to, near the end, when he had been out exploring. Someone who had a last, or lasting maybe, reminiscence of him — however small. A bit of information beyond the bag of meaningless things the police brought. Something personal, beyond the facts of what had happened to Bliss in the end. After a year of living without Bliss, that was how my mother said she could try to settle it in her mind and move forward. I guess my way was to follow a memory, a spirit, into the woods. My parents looked for a trace of him still there; I looked for a trace of him still here.

I have to finally accept that Bliss did end it all on purpose. He went. He saw. He explored. But then? For now, I can only think of how the ghost of Speckles leapt into the boneyard.

I can't hold on anymore to the thought that Bliss was simply crossing the overpass to come home when it happened. That he was turning around, coming back to us. I can't make myself think any longer that maybe he had stepped on the railing at the side of the roadway to look back, up high to have a perfect view at how far he'd come, but then he simply stumbled. No, I know that wasn't it. Just like I know now that I couldn't have stopped him from going in the first place. I can't blame myself for thinking I should have.

But that doesn't mean his death wasn't an accident. It was. It was because of something beyond his control, started long ago, by the illness inside him, by the ever-returning darkness, that pulled him down so far it ultimately felt inescapable. He didn't decide his own end; it's the same as if he was claimed by a horrible disease. Going elsewhere, seeing different scenery, hearing different sounds, breathing different air didn't change the way his brain worked, didn't cure him. But he had exhausted everything he could think of. I will always believe, in fact I know, that he tried. He tried so hard to be happy, to escape the sadness, to leave every bad thought behind.

And it was a tragedy. Forever was changed in an instant. I have learned that from the boneyard. A deer is not a man, but it can happen that quickly. A buck can leap in front of a car. Bliss decided to take a step. An intentional final step. A step out. Step off. Step away. Finally so far away.

My parents came home from their supposed *vacation* — their time to get away together. Refreshed. Heads cleared. No one around here will ever be told any different. The only people who really know why they were gone are me and Jill (and Johnny) and Dean. My parents felt no need to try to explain anything else anymore.

The waitress my parents talked to remembered Bliss because he was cute, she said. She figured they were around the same age and she had never met anyone from New Brunswick before. That is the sum total of it. The restaurant was a seasonal roadside place called E.Z.'s Eats and Treats. Mom and Dad sat quietly in a booth there and had a coffee and stared out the window a while. I don't know if the waitress asked why my parents wanted to know about Bliss, or what they said, but now her memory is my parents' memory as well — and mine too, I guess. I'm glad to know that before the end, Bliss did get to have some time exploring. He had made it well into Ontario.

Foster buried Speckles. Right where he was, under the tree. He could have tossed him in the boneyard, or left him, but he didn't. Foster made him a twig-art grave marker as well. It was a simple cross twisted with a heart and antlers, like the top of Foster's massive twig throne. Foster showed it to me the last time he brought down a load of tables.

I was sitting on the picnic table at the barn with Dean. I knew what it was right away.

"For your hart," Foster said and held it up.

"It's perfect," I said.

The movers delivered all the items from the Vaughn estate to the store. The Room was pretty much empty so we put the things that wouldn't fit in the regular storage room in there. Quinny finally saw the inside of it. I could tell she was disappointed. Dad asked Quinny and Elizabeth to come sort it all with me, Dean and my mother. Dad let each of us take something free-of-charge before it was all offered for sale. Quinny chose a beautiful cast iron Victorian plant stand with a scene of a sailboat on the top. Elizabeth chose a bedside rocker. Dean chose the flame birch dresser to give to Jill and Johnny for their house, which was very sweet. My mother said she didn't need anything. Dad didn't take anything but kept a box of books for Foster. He also chose a lovely tall crystal vase for Cecil's wife Mavis. I asked to keep a few of Ivy Vaughn's dishes from the rainbow room so I can recreate part of her display in my bedroom window after Community Days are done.

We shuffled things around on the sales floor so that the entire estate contents would fit at once. Quinny passed the news around Riverbend that on Saturday we'd have everything out. We moved it all on Friday night after closing. I've never seen the barn so full. My father marked every price tag of a piece from the cottage with a little blue dot. It wouldn't mean anything to the tourists or arouse any additional interest, but locals knew that was the secret code. Dad priced things reasonably too. I know he could have made more money, but it was his way of sharing the estate with everyone, satisfying the curiosity they all had — wanting to know what had sat in that cottage, nearby all those years, but locked away.

My father opened the doors an hour early and people came in and bought their piece of local history. It was like a Riverbend reunion at The Purple Barn. All our regular customers came — Lolly Perkins, Mrs. Harris and the rest — as well as some people I'm sure had never been in the store before. Quinny's husband George came. I assured him his secret was safe, and I told him that I was a big fan of his gorgeous quilts. Mom served lemonade even and set out plates of cookies. It was fun. Like a party. I think Ivy Vaughn would have loved it. Everything was pretty much gone by closing. It was a record sales total for us for a single day.

My father kept out the two thousand dollars he had spent to buy the things, then set the rest aside in a bank account for the high school. It is to be used for two new annual memorial scholarships given at graduation — one for Kevin Vaughn and one for Bliss. They are to be granted each year to students who will be attending university in Fredericton. It's where Dean will go back for his second year in the fall and where I'll start too, taking an arts degree with some history courses until I decide any different. Dean has already figured out that his apartment is only a fifteen-minute walk from the residence I'll be staying in.

I packed up Bliss's room. My parents agreed it was time. I touched his things, lifted and moved them from the last place he had put them. For everything in his room I know the meaning, the memory that went with it. I know which things he liked, and why, where he got them — whether as a gift or something he bought himself.

But still these are things and not Bliss. He is so strong in my mind I don't need an object to remind me of him.

I did keep his books of licence plate rubbings. His hands had smoothed those pages, back and forth with the crayon again and again, making an imprint of a place he'd never been. And as he was doing it, I was his lookout, keeping him safe. Even now the wax on the paper is sleek, made so by his hand working across each page. The licence plate books are made of memories of a whole collection of people who visited our place, out exploring on their summer vacations. And they hold memories of Bliss and me too, not a souvenir of a single time, but years of our time.

My mother wanted his pictures, and old school books, report cards and sports medals, because those are things she would have kept whether he was here with us or not. But his clothes were donated to the church, and the few posters from his room were taken down. Everything else he owned was gathered up. It is a tribute to him to show that we have the power to let them go.

I packed them, boxed them, and we are going to burn them in a big bonfire behind the barn. The flames will climb high and the smoke will fill the air. The tiniest bits of ash will lift and carry and perhaps fall like snowflakes over the boneyard.

Acknowledgements

Thank you to my agent, Hilary McMahon, for her usual enthusiasm and for getting this whole thing started.

Thank you to my editor, Bethany Gibson, for asking me all the right questions and for being so smart, patient and kind.

Thank you to everyone at the wonderful Goose Lane Editions for all doing what you do best to produce this finished book.

To the Canada Council for the Arts, my sincere appreciation for awarding me a Creation Grant to work on this novel.

Thank you to everyone in the literary and arts communities who has been encouraging and supportive of what I do.

To my parents, Fredrica and David Givan, thank you for raising me in Hawkshaw, New Brunswick, and for letting me explore our endless backyard forest. I know my appreciation of nature came from you two.

And finally to Shane and Eli and Tess: love you always.

RIEL NASON is the author of *The Town That Drowned,* which won both the 2012 Commonwealth Book Prize for Canada and Europe and the 2012 Margaret and John Savage First Book Award. The novel was also a finalist for several other awards, in addition to being longlisted for the 2013 International IMPAC Dublin Literary Award.

Riel was a professional antique dealer for many years and for more than a decade wrote a column on collectibles for New Brunswick's *Telegraph-Journal.* As well as being a writer, she is an acclaimed textile artist. Riel lives in Quispamsis, New Brunswick, with her family.